Resident Aliens

RESIDENT ALIENS

A NOVEL

Joe Ashby Porter

NEW AMSTERDAM BOOKS
IVAN R. DEE, PUBLISHER
CHICAGO

RESIDENT ALIENS. Copyright © 2000 by Joe Ashby Porter. All rights reserved, including the right to reproduce this book or portions thereof in any form. For information, address: Ivan R. Dee, Publisher, 1332 North Halsted Street, Chicago 60622. Manufactured in the United States of America and printed on acid-free paper.

Library of Congress Cataloging-in-Publication Data:
Porter, Joseph Ashby, 1942–
    Resident aliens / Joe Ashby Porter.
      p. cm.
      ISBN 1-56663-332-X (alk. paper)
      1. Charlottesville (Va.)—Fiction.   2. Aliens—Fiction.   I. Title.
PS3566.O6515 R47 2000
813'.54—dc21   00-024072

For Yves

I

"WE'RE OFF ANYWAY," said Chantal. "I think it won't rain after all, either. What time is it?" She drove smoothly, well over the legal limit, on the deserted four-lane freeway that led from Charlottesville, Virginia, east to the ocean. "What time is it, I said."

"Oh. Four," said Jean-Luc, still pale and in a funk. "I didn't hear. Sorry, Chantal, about everything. I didn't know what to do, it was horrible. You were wonderful. The car seems okay. . . ."

"If she'd done serious damage we'd know by now, wouldn't we?"

Jean-Luc stared out the open window at rolling picture-book pastures, black-and-white cattle flashing past. He sighed and began to relax and recover himself. It was a pleasant September afternoon in 1974. It would be a pleasant weekend with Chantal. The beach should be pleasant now that the season was over. "If repairs have to be made, I'll pay of course. She really goes crazy sometimes lately, it's outrageous. She didn't use to be like that at all. The worst is, I can't see a way out. She no longer seems able to talk to me like a civilized adult. She won't talk lightly, you know? I try to talk about things that are objectively interesting, impersonal things, but she'll only talk more bullshit like what you witnessed today, and I apologize again. That's why she's always after me to go off and be alone with her: so we can 'work it through' or whatever. She's *always* rabid when she gets me alone. Invariably, like you saw her today. Can you imagine? I'm afraid of her sometimes, that violence, and I hate it so I, well, my stomach's still in knots. Ugh!"

"I don't see how you bear it."

"Me neither!"

"I don't see *why* you bear it, Jean-Luc. How long is it you've been married?"

"Centuries! Seven years, I think, but we lived together five or six before that. But it's only the past year she's been like this, and only since I met you that it's been so unrelenting. I . . . oh let's not talk about Irène now! Hungry? We could pull off somewhere."

"I'd rather not. These woods look as if they might be infested with red-throats."

"Necks."

"I would like a pear though. Maybe a sandwich too. We split one?"

"Good, here."

"Thanks. Mmm, delicious. If you move your seat back you'll be more comfortable, Jean-Luc."

"I would. It's as far back as it was intended to go already, though. Oh well. How are your courses? Or is it too early to tell."

"Unfortunately nothing's going to be as good as you were. Also I'm beginning to wonder whether my advantage might somehow prove null. By all rights I should be leading the pack. If you heard, well of course you do hear what they do to our poor language, even the best of them, even the ones that've spent a summer in Dijon. Yet it's as if the faculty has agreed to solve the problem by contriving ingenious approaches that accommodate garbling and misunderstanding. You know?"

"Steel yourself. Did you see me wince once, all summer?"

"I saw your eyes sparkle rather frequently."

"None of your fellows did though, Chantal. And some of those sparkles had nothing to do with their manglings. I dreamed about you, literally. Several times, too."

"No. . . ."

"I did, Chantal. Wet dreams. The first time it happened I was intrigued but the second time I was dumbfounded. It was unprecedented for my dreams to be so single-minded."

"Do you still . . . ?"

"I wish. Not that I'd rather find you in a dream than in reality. But I like you there too, I wish I could have you both places. I love you, Chantal."

"Tell me how old you are then."

"Why are you so curious? What difference does it make?"

"None to me, Jean-Luc. You're the one who seems to think it's important, hiding it."

"I know it's silly. Okay, thirty-five. Are you reeling?"

"I wouldn't reel if you told me you'd had your thirty-eighth birthday last January."

"What?"

"It's on your driver's license."

"Are you angry?"

"Of course not. Light me a cigarette, would you?"

"It's that I hate age, I mean I—here Chantal, cigarette —I hate the idea of always being one specific age. It's demeaning. I don't want to be some age other than thirty-eight—I just chose thirty-five at random—"

"Oh?"

"Well, I wanted it to be plausible as well as false, of course, so I wouldn't have said twelve or three hundred. Good point. Anyway I don't want to be thirty-five any more than thirty-eight. I don't want to be *any* age. Because people worry about it, print it on driver's licenses as if it were a characteristic worth noting! Frankly, Chantal, I've never happened to be the lover of anyone nearly so much my junior as you. But I don't find myself thinking much about it. Do you? Do you think we're ill-matched? Let me know, by the way, when you want me to drive."

"I wanted to know, that's all. I was a bit surprised—I'd thought you were thirty-one or -two."

"Even after the first morning you woke up with me in your bed?"

"How old is Irène, Jean-Luc?"

"I don't know. I mean she's about forty-two months younger than I, so sometimes she comes out three years younger, sometimes four. But you see? You're just like other people, you're obsessed with ages. Admit it, it's a common enough failing, I can take it in stride. What are you thinking?"

"Oh, about what a bore graduate study is in Mr. Jefferson's academical village and everywhere else, how dreary and out-of-touch. But I don't want that to make me do it badly. I may chuck it but so long as I haven't I want to do it well. And that's to say I'll have my hands fairly full in the next few months. I was thinking about that and, with respect to that, whether I should move into your house. Then I thought, why doesn't Jean-Luc move in with me?"

"It would be wonderful. . . ." Jean-Luc was angular and dark. He leaned against the headrest, smiling with his eyes closed, and rubbed a thumb knuckle of the hand holding the cigarette lightly back and forth over his thick handsome moustache. "We could do anything we wanted."

"I.e., no." Chantal was small and thin, with delicate bones. Behind her sunglasses were luminous brown eyes with dark circles under them. She looked like a child pretending to drive. The Japanese automobile's steering wheel looked absurdly large in her hands. When Jean-Luc had first seen her she had reminded him a little of Piaf—he had called three of her favorite movie stars to her mind. At the beginning of the summer she had come from Montréal, her birthplace and home until then, to Virginia to begin work toward a doctorate in French literature, and had enrolled in two of the four available courses all taught by Jean-Luc who alone in the department had been braving the wretched wet heat of the Charlottesville summer. Piaf and the three handsome movie stars had assisted at an evening's flirtation and lingered through part of a night of intermittent fucking and dozing and then had departed since they were no longer needed. Jean-Luc smoothed his moustache and thought of the pleasures living alone with Chantal would afford. Like a sultan he would be able to feel her up, strip and fuck her whenever he wished. He had missed her during the three weeks she had been back with her parents. "I meant to ask, Chantal: how was the trip from Montréal? I wish I could have met your plane."

"It wasn't bad."

"Tell."

"Tell what? I was thinking about you the whole time, the planes were the usual, the airports earnest bad taste everywhere. I had to wait an hour and a half in Washington. That, as a matter of fact, was the least unpleasant leg of the journey. I sat at the counter in the airport restaurant and looked at a U.S. newspaper. There was a young man next to me reading—trying to read—something in French about desire and revolution. . . ."

"Attractive?"

"?"

"The desiring young revolutionary."

"Oh, I suppose—unkempt, wire-rimmed glasses, you know, Levi's. He seemed to be underscoring words he wasn't sure of, and for some he'd consult one of those pocket Larousses. His difficulty seemed extreme, every third word was underscored. Do you suppose he intended to go back and learn them one by one? Seems inefficient."

"Indeed. Might have done better to read through his Larousse."

"Except he did seem to be reading with some comprehension. Enjoyment even. From time to time he'd stop and be lost in thought or rapture or both, sipping coffee, his eyes shining. But only for a few seconds, then back to work. There was something about him, Jean-Luc, about the whole scene, fat businessmen taking a lively interest in the financial pages of their papers and all eating the sugariest desserts methodically and without tasting, and then lots of teenagers lounging and posing with their musical comedy clothes, all drinking Coca-Colas and chewing ice. A stout matron at the cash register with an orchid corsage taking her work very seriously, waitresses who hadn't taken anything seriously in forty years. Everything fitted in the worst way, seamless, except for the boy next to me. What was he doing there? His industry so surpassed mine I gave up, pretended to keep reading but really watched him surreptitiously—not that he was likely to notice anything other than his book and whatever he saw when his eyes shone. I just watched him and the place and tried to put them together. Because the incongruity was dismaying me, giving me feelings of slippage. Time was running out too. I really half believed that unless I could resolve or make sense of it something terrible, the plane would crash or I don't know, something, you can't imagine how it felt. But then—not a minute too soon either, I almost missed the plane—he and the place clicked. Not only was he not incongruous, I realized the place would've been incomplete, unthinkable without its young man reading about revolution and desire in a language not his own. There were no seams at all. I ran for my plane."

"The young man didn't come too? I was thinking he could've been one of my students, one of your classmates."

"It would be funny, wouldn't it. No. Or if my plane was his he missed it for having his head in the clouds. Oh dear, Jean-Luc, I. . . ."

"It's okay, never mind. Here, my handkerchief. Okay? Want me to drive? You know, I love you so much I can hardly believe it, I worship your nooky, baby."

"I don't mind driving. Maybe you want to, though. Jean-Luc . . . ?"

"Yes?"

"Was Irène born in Brittany too?"

"Provence. Toulon, the section they call Chicago. Ever been there?"

"No."

"It's an older section down near the water. Like Marseille—tamer but, you know, prostitutes, sailors, spicy crime. Not large though. Irène was born there. She likes to give the impression that her mother was a prostitute and her father a seafaring customer, but in fact her parents were fishmongers, honest and hardworking. Later with savings they bought a little farm at a village not far inland, when Irène was five or six. She spent her girlhood there. Her father whom she adored died when she was nine. Her mother, for whom she had a sort of guarded respect, lived on there until three years ago when she died. I visited her several times with Irène. I liked her very much indeed and I think she approved of me in spite of my seeming, to her, somewhat laughable, insubstantial, frivolous. She enjoyed laughing at demonstrations of my lack of good provincial solidity and I loved her to laugh at me. Her name was Eulalie. In time she wanted me to call her that, but I never could quite bring myself to do it. Look, Chantal! There!"

"What?"

"Too late. It was a deer."

"Good heavens, really? Here?"

"Yes, yes, Chantal. You see signs on the freeway that say 'Deer Crossing.'"

"It's incredible." After a moment she said, "Did you work on your book while I was away?"

"I don't want to talk about it."

"Jean-Luc, you wouldn't really move in with me, would you? Out of the question, no?"

"Oh Chantal, wouldn't it be wonderful if life were simpler."

"Why not, though. I see that you and Irène must have been perfection for each other once upon a time. But now you only seem to get in each other's way. I've never seen so little love in a supposedly intimate relationship between adults as intelligent and even well-meaning as you both are. Mutual abuse is about all there seems to be. Then why keep it up? I think it would be better for her too, a release. Your marriage is spinning its wheels, and the spinning makes movement increasingly less likely. You should get out and walk. I don't know, it does seem so, Jean-Luc. Have I said too much?"

"No, no. No. Of course not."

"Then?"

Jean-Luc sighed, a quizzical smile on his handsome weary face. His eyes went blank. Chantal drove without speaking. Jean-Luc sighed again. "I don't know, Chantal. If anything you're glossing over the awfulness of the situation and sometimes, especially lately, I fear that what you say is the whole truth, or all that matters. But I'm not convinced. I'm not and even if I were I'm not sure I'd be able to leave her, I don't know. If she left me, yes, I could accept it. Even now I wish she'd go away for a while. I suggested it, maybe she will—if only for a month, it would give me breathing space. I know I've wounded her and I regret it more than anything and I'm not likely to forget, she's such a blackmailer, but *I didn't do it intentionally* and nothing I've done warrants my finding myself in a new nightmare every time I turn a corner. It isn't fair at all. Where's justice? When I was a lad I counted on justice's being a part of the order of things."

"Justice, Jean-Luc?"

"Imagine."

"What does Irène think about my coming to live at your house?"

"She suggested it—I didn't dare. She said you might 'grow up a little' there. Indeed you might. I don't know, Chantal. Of course it could prove a horror show but then you, at any rate, can always leave. But I do think it might work. At the moment anyway I think it looks more workable and saner than the alternative, our visiting each other continually, with all the fuss that would entail."

"And Mouse?"

"What do you mean?"

"What does she think of the idea?"

"I don't know that Irène's suggested it to her—I haven't. She'd probably be pleased, you know. Anyway Mouse'll go along with whatever Irène wants. What do *you* think of the idea?"

"I'd have to find someone to take my apartment, move out everything. I don't know though. I'd be readier if there were another male there, it would feel healthier. I don't know, I'm inclined to say yes too, Jean-Luc. But why don't we let it ride for a week, say, think more."

"Fine."

"How did Irène's mother die?"

"Sleeping. Without preceding illness. She was found the next morning by a crony. I hope my parents are as lucky."

"Mine too."

"By the way, Chantal, did you tell your parents about us?"

"You and me? Sort of."

"How'd they react?"

"They wondered if I didn't perhaps think someone nearer my own age might be more suitable, though they assured me I was old enough to think for myself."

A hitchhiker stood near where a small road gave onto the freeway. The terrain was lowering and flattening, yellowing. Jean-Luc was accustomed to riding in small cars, he seldom noticed the discomfort. Chantal's petit bourgeois parents aside, Irène aside, Jean-Luc was still more dubious than he let show about the affair he was having with Chantal. It was good for her of course—her few previous romances had been wastes of time at best, foolish masquerades with empty-headed boys who understood less than nothing about making love. Chantal was good for Jean-Luc too. The directness and simplicity of loving her was miraculous and like fresh air to someone lost in a mine. Yet Jean-Luc wondered whether he might not somehow be compromising and deceiving himself, playing a shameful escapist sort of game by ignoring and overlooking more than was conscionable. For instance, how intelligent was Chantal, after all? Wasn't she possibly even a bit stupid? Had Jean-Luc convinced himself that she was more attractive than she really was? There was traffic now. An airy copse glided past.

"I'd have given him a ride if I were alone—but we wouldn't have been able to talk, you and I."

"Mmm, or...." Jean-Luc leaned over and kissed Chantal slowly behind her ear.

"Your moustache tickles. Oh, Jean-Luc, I thought we wouldn't ever get away, I thought she wasn't going to give up when I saw her face under the hood and the way she was monkeying with the engine."

"She doesn't know beans about cars, either—luckily, I suppose. Except that she might unintentionally have done serious expensive damage if we'd let her go on."

"I felt trapped, and then when she said, 'By the way, I've let the air out of the tires,' it all seemed hopeless and pathetic and sordid. I hated her at that moment more than I've ever hated anybody."

"I could have killed her, I was so angry—except who knew what she might do next, she was so irrational. She was berserk, Chantal. Just before we left, though, when she came out again—you were inside—she seemed to have come out of it, to be a little contrite. But, my god, the spectacle of *her* accusing *you* of destroying things as she disembowelled your poor car—it was unnerving."

"And doesn't it occur to her that with Mouse there she hasn't a leg to stand on? Doesn't she think about glass houses?"

"Not Irène. Though I must say Mouse was a help today."

"She reined Irène in more than you did, Jean-Luc."

"I know and I'm grateful, however it infuriates me to see her heeded after I've been ignored and worse."

"But what's the difference, so long as we escaped unharmed? I think I like Mouse."

"I don't. But let that pass. Know what first attracted me to you, Chantal?"

"No."

"Me neither. I wish I did, it might be useful."

"How? I can see that it might be useful to me. . . . What will attract you to me last, do you suppose?"

"Last? Cruelty perhaps, inaccessibility, indifference. Assuming there *is* a last. All in due course though, all in good time. I'll tell you what attracts me to you now."

"I'd like to hear."

"Everything, including the way you keep shifting your little ass around to find a comfortable position and the creaminess of your amazing skin, and how brave and resolute you are. I haven't felt this way since I was twenty, Chantal. I love it, I can't get enough, it's incredible."

"Isn't it."

"I love it."

"Jean-Luc? What . . . what class do you come from? Are your parents rich?"

Jean-Luc laughed. "Listen, Chantal: Irène for some reason is convinced your family is very wealthy. She thinks of it as a trump card against you. She's saving it, but when she talks to me about you it's one of the things she touches on most darkly."

"You don't set her straight?"

"But she doesn't believe me. Listen: you know you made a couple of calls to your parents from our house? So the number was listed on the bill. So Irène investigated somehow and informed me that anyone with that number has to live in an extremely expensive quarter of Montréal."

"She should see. But maybe the same prefix covers other neighborhoods. We should arrange for her to see a photo of my parents' house."

"She'd detect the contrivance and not believe it was your parents' house at all. Even if she visited them she might think it some ruse—a front we had arranged, actors in a rented house. A nose keen as hers can sniff out fraud anywhere."

"Whew! I guess we don't try disabusing her then."

"No percentage."

"But tell me about your parents—don't only rich families send their children to the Lycée Condorcet? Proust went there."

"Rich? It depends on what you mean. From what I know of your parents, I imagine they'd think mine rich. My parents don't think of themselves that way though. They think of themselves as old-fashioned, proper and ordinary. In terms of liquid cash and convertible assets, I don't really know. If Father were a specialist with a fancy clientele he might be very wealthy, but he's basically just a general practitioner of a sort that's disappearing in Paris, his clientele is heterogeneous and a fair portion of his work has been without fee. I think it's the sleep cure, what he comes closest to specializing in, that brings in the most money for the least effort. I'd estimate, I don't know, three-quarters of a million dollars, maybe. They live frugally in a good house they've had for half a century, they only had one child, their annual vacations—Étretat in August and Cavalaire in the spring—are modest. You see? They live far beneath their means, in the old way. I never thought of them as wealthy. It's true Irène bristled and rattled sabers when she first met them, but she's come to like and even admire them, especially Father. Her mother and they hit it off perfectly the first and only time they met, at our wedding. Thereafter she always wanted to hear from us about how they were, they always inquired after her; and I think the mutual affection always grew and in fact assumed phenomenal proportions, perhaps precisely because they never did see each other again."

"They came for her funeral?"

"No, but they wish they'd been able."

"How often do you see them?"

"Once a year for a week or so. I wish it could be more, I miss them, Father anyway."

"Here?"

"There, always. They wouldn't come here for anything, not even if I were dying, I think. I can't say I blame them either. You know a few years ago Irène and I began to see that after all we wouldn't before long be returning to France to live. We'd become expatriates almost without noticing, and the condition was permanent. That discovery was unpleasant and at the time some of my discomfort expressed itself in resentment at my parents' refusal to visit here. But that changed. Now I think they're right and wise."

"Irène's mother never came either, I suppose."

"No. There was even less question of her coming. Though she in fact would have been amused, I think, if she'd come."

"Jean-Luc, Jean-Luc, I love to hear about these things. But sometimes, I don't know, it saddens me to think that what you tell me is a tiny fraction of what Irène knows about you. You ought at least to tell me some things anyway that she doesn't know, and promise never to tell her. It wouldn't begin to redress the imbalance, but it'd be appreciated as a gesture of good faith. Kiss me."

"Where?"

"Where you please so long as you don't block my vision or interfere with my steering hands or my accelerating or braking or merely speed-maintaining foot. I—mmm, thanks, that's where I secretly hoped you'd do it, you rascal—I must remember, by the way, to pay you for those calls home, the ones Irène investigated. Really, if I'm to come to live in your house we must be fastidious about money."

"Ugh. But you're right. Are you wearing any underpants?"

"Yes. You?"

"No, as it happens."

"Jean-Luc, will there be old hotels at the beach? If there are let's stay in one."

"Okay. Chantal! The fuel gauge reads empty!"

"Good heavens. I'll pull in there then—I need to pee anyway. But Jean-Luc, would you deal with the attendant? Their English is still a strain for me and it takes forever for them to understand me."

A few minutes later they were back on the freeway. Jean-Luc was driving. Chantal turned on the radio at a low volume, almost inaudible, the way she liked it. How much farther? Was there a hint of seawater in the air? Jean-Luc drove faster than Chantal had done.

Mouse—she had used the direct translation of her Oneida name, Otsinowa, since childhood—ambled down the hill through sunlight and shadows, kicking sticks and enrinded black walnuts out of her path. Thin as she was, with her long lustrous coarse black hair, brown skin, wide dark eyes, she was beautiful and seemed unconscious of it now as always. She shuffled in the front doorway and up the stair without a word, into her room and slammed the door after her, to show she was displeased. As if it made any difference. A sweet compliance suited her better. In fits of pique when she fancied herself dignified she was in fact ridiculous. Let her sulk and stew, there'd be no apologies. And the wonder of it was, Mouse would come out of it soon anyway. She could be counted on. Irène prepared a cup of instant coffee, her tenth of the day. At the kitchen table she lit a cigarette and shook open *Le Monde.*

For the last half hour she had felt a surprising calm and assurance. Maybe she had gone into overdrive, maybe her consciousness had taken a quantum leap. Even when she had been shouting at Jean-Luc, the pig, insisting that he not go away with Chantal for the weekend, her shouts had been without rancor, she had felt a smooth transcendence of the immediate local circumstance. She had noticed that she was not grimacing as would have been expected. These two pieces of shit had been contorting their visages in the ugliest wildest fashions. She would like it to have been filmed so that she could show them. She would like to have arranged for it to be beamed at their little love-nest so that when they finished their smarming and Jean-Luc switched on the television set they would see themselves in full sordid craziness. Oh well. Irène stirred her coffee. "Remember who you are," she said to herself. At the other end of the long kitchen wrens squabbled in the ivy that grew over the windows there.

It was a genial room, untidy and not very clean. Old newspapers and magazines collected in a corner until someone bothered to move them to a larger and less frequently troubled collection on the back porch. Soiled dishes collected in the sink, in the dishwasher that didn't work, on counters, tables, atop the refrigerator, until somebody bothered to wash them. Messages stayed on the makeshift bulletin board among photographs and newspaper articles for months, until the thumbtacks holding them in place were needed for something else. Garbage collected in brown paper grocery bags and seeped through onto the linoleum, ashes and butts collected in oyster shells and overflowed. There were bouquets of immortelles in clay pots.

The house had begun as an ordinary on the stage route between Washington and Charlottesville. Later paved roads followed different courses and the ordinary became a private dwelling, a very isolated one. Even now no others could be seen from it. A new gravel road some three kilometers long was laid, to connect the house down a cleared hillside, across a brook, uphill through woods, with the nearest paved road. Most of the original building had remained intact through waves of neglect and repair, though the kitchen with its many windows and the porches were added. Irène and Jean-Luc had chosen the house not so much for its seclusion or its age (though they valued both) as for its situation between Charlottesville where Jean-Luc taught and Washington where nearly all Irène's work as reporter and correspondent for *Le Monde* had to be done. The hour's drive either way was cumbersome but manageable. It was a distance that kept friends and acquaintances from making nuisances of themselves, while allowing them usually to come when invited. And when they were there they felt privileged because of the time and effort the visit had cost them.

    Irène sat with legs crossed, one elbow on the table, drinking coffee. She was not thin as in their various ways Jean-Luc, Chantal and Mouse all were. Her body was trim and firm like a dancer's, and well-proportioned except for her shortish legs. Now she was barefoot and wore a denim wrap-around skirt and a black turtleneck jersey. From the neck up Irène was arresting in person though not in photographs, where she seemed to fade or lose focus. For more than a decade she had worn her grey-blonde hair in the classic French intellectual and artistic woman's short bob with bangs. Her face was arresting because of her high and rather narrow cheekbones, because of her strong unadorned mouth and her long blunt nose, and most because of what she did with her pale blue eyes behind her large wire-rimmed spectacles. Casual acquaintances sometimes remembered Irène as mildly cross-eyed, though she was not at all so, because Irène's eyes never seemed to be seeing or looking at anything. The lenses of her spectacles were slightly tinted a neutral color and were so large that they would have more than served for a second pair of eyes below Irène's own. She never seemed quite to see anything and in particular never seemed quite to look at any person, at least not in a way that implied recognition. The effect was like feeling the wandering gaze of a two-month-old pass across one's face. In repose the lenses of her spectacles seemed too heavy for the delicate frame because the tinting gave them a quality like that of thick leaded glass, but any motion revealed that they were alarmingly thin to be so large, thin as the most fragile blown glass. In fact the lenses were not glass but a tough plastic. The tint was photosensitive, increasing to protect the eyes from increasing intensities of light. When Irène was near another person, near enough to touch, engaged in conversation, she characteristically kept her eyes and lids somewhat lowered. Instead of looking into the other's eyes she seemed to look into the mouth or at the chin, though it was difficult to be quite sure since the pale blue and thus the direction of her look was half hidden under sandy lashes that were extraordinarily thick though not long. Though in these moments she did give at least the impression of addressing other people's mouths, whenever her glance strayed above the ends of their noses it was quick and idle and seemed not to have happened, like those glances by which one may evaluate a friend's coiffure without seeming to. Irène's eyes played these tricks even when she was speaking most openly and urgently, when the plucked sandy brows were at their most expressive. They played other tricks too.

"She gives herself away, Jean-Luc," Irène said in her mind. Fairly often conversations with other people amounting to monologues occurred in Irène's mind, and occasionally turns of phrase from these monologues would later make their way into actual conversations with the imagined listener. "It's astonishing, Jean-Luc. You remember, when she was protecting her little vehicle from me as if it were a matter of life and death? 'You stay away from my car!' she said, and she would have assaulted me if I'd touched that piece of machinery again—what kind of value system does that manifest, by the way! I said, '*You* stay away from my husband and my house!' The glazed look of blank stupidity settled on her face. I tried to get through, I said, 'You can't just waltz in and destroy things, Chantal. You can't.' And then do you remember what she said? She said, 'Why don't you let him decide.' It's amazing. She wasn't saying I should let (as if it's a question of my 'letting' you do anything) you decide whether to run off for a hideous little tryst with her, no, she was saying I should 'let' you decide whether she could *'waltz in and destroy everything.'* The more I thought about it afterwards the more ominous it seemed. I begin to wonder if half the thrill for her might not be the hope of destroying something fine that's survived all other onslaughts. I'm almost afraid to hear her say anything now, for fear she'll give away intentions and assumptions that are still worse." Irène gave a little nod with raised eyebrows for emphasis, and turned rattling pages of the newspaper.

Jean-Luc had returned from his last Friday afternoon class, driven by Chantal since his car was at a garage being tuned. He had walked into the kitchen where Irène and Mouse were, and said, "Hi. Guess what? I'm going to the beach." Meanwhile Chantal had entered the house after him and gone directly up to his room to collect some of her things for the trip. Irène was tired. She had been to Washington every day that week, and she had counted on a comparatively peaceful weekend in which, even if Chantal were there the whole time and even if Mouse was fretful, she and her husband would be able to spend a few hours alone together. Irène had worked herself into a mood of reconciliation and acceptance, and since the middle of the week she had been unusually attentive to Mouse so that Mouse wouldn't resent Irène's being alone with Jean-Luc during the weekend. It had been a rude shock when Jean-Luc had announced his plan. "Is everybody invited?" Irène had asked.

Jean-Luc had said, "No," lightly with characteristic timid bravado that was one of the most loveable things about him and one of the most infuriating. Irène loved him, his timid bravado embarrassed her, made her feel ashamed of herself and him and for the moment she could say nothing more than, "Stay, don't go," even though seconds before a rancorous verbal storm had been brewing. He went upstairs to pack, Mouse had said nothing, as had come to be her habit in the confrontations between Irène and Jean-Luc which made her, Mouse, so unhappy she wanted to put her hands over her ears and die or run away, so unhappy she felt as if she actually were dying and she wanted not to love Irène, wanted somehow to stop loving her. Mouse sat very still and looked at her knees. She was not trying to show anything, but Irène felt it and felt guilty of it. She walked into the hallway. Jean-Luc and Chantal were upstairs talking in undertones, packing what they needed for the weekend—Jean-Luc wanted to slip away as quickly as possible. Mouse sat in the kitchen, miserable, thinking that if Jean-Luc and Chantal did change their plans and stay it would be unbearable because they would soon feel themselves imprisoned and turn resentful but since they wouldn't, since Jean-Luc wouldn't knuckle under now to Irène Mouse was thinking that the whole weekend Irène would be crazily bitter and resentful with her mind always on Jean-Luc and no place in her heart for Mouse.

Mouse sat back in the kitchen, Jean-Luc and Chantal bustled about discreetly overhead. Irène stood in the hallway by the stair and held to one of the balusters. Her mouth opened as if she were about to say "Ah..." and then say something else. Then she went outside and let the air out of the tires of Chantal's car. She did it not because she imagined it might prevent Jean-Luc's and Chantal's departure but because she wanted to gain time to say more to Jean-Luc. And that it was a clownish sort of thing to do seemed to the good: it should make her seem a little ridiculous, someone to laugh at not flee—it might reduce the tension and allow them all to relax.

As the air hissed from the nozzles the car itself had seemed to relax and settle down tire by tire like a camel for a rest, and Irène had then begun to notice her own unprecedented ease and freedom from anger and bitterness. When all the tires were quite flat she had opened the hood intending to remove and hide some part of the engine for good measure, and she had been trying to deduce which of the separable parts was, unlike the dipstick, vital when Jean-Luc and Chantal had stepped out of the house with their picnic basket and suitcase. Irène had looked up at them for a moment with a vague sociable demeanor, as if they were passers-by and she a busy mechanic, and then she had put her head back under the hood.

Chantal had clearly been furious, though she had said no more than, "Stay away from my car," and "Why don't you let him decide," before she stalked inside to telephone someone who came fifteen minutes later with a small tank of compressed air. Jean-Luc seemed to have been too astonished to be very angry, though he had as by reflex gone through some of the motions of anger. "This is outrageous," he had said.

"You weren't giving me a chance to say two words before you zipped off to the beach," Irène had said, and she had proceeded to make full use of the time gained, talking to Jean-Luc in the bright sunshine and inside when he retreated there, following him from room to room, and then again outside when he oversaw the re-filling of the tires. Jean-Luc in an unprecedented move had appealed to Mouse for support, and Mouse had ventured a few enjoinders like, "Be sensible, Irène," a few expressions of a sort of maternal disapproval. Irène had paid her no more mind than she had paid the service station attendant who had said nothing and had pretended to be utterly absorbed in his chore. She had used the half hour she had gained by following Jean-Luc and speaking loudly, rapidly, eloquently without anger in her flat unmusical voice. Jean-Luc had not risen to the occasion, Irène now thought, but he had not quite disgraced himself either. Turning the pages of *Le Monde* she was remembering the Jean-Luc of an hour before. He was beautiful, it was much too late now for her to find, see, any other man nearly as beautiful. Through twelve years in her eyes his beauty had increased steadily and relentlessly as his age. With his age, in his aging. The little he had said—"This is outrageous," and "If you'd do this" (let the air out of Chantal's tires) "what might you not do? Did you know I have nightmares about you?" and "Your tactics are self-defeating. You must see that you've made it impossible for me to stay now"—had been beside the point, lame and ridiculous except for when he had gotten out of the car whose engine Chantal had already started and come back into the house, into the kitchen where Irène was already making as if to read the newspaper and simply said, "See you Sunday, Irène," and kissed her head, in her hair. But his expressions and gestures, his movements and stances had been fine as could be. All his nocturnal grace had been there, his softness and solemnity, his hesitations and graceful breakings-off. Irène tilted up her coffee cup. "Remember how lucky you are," she warned herself.

Mouse and Irène had met about two years before in Washington, and they had quickly fallen in love, into a love fraught with hindrances and contradictions. They had met by chance—by a series of chances—one morning on Pennsylvania Avenue outside the high fence around the White House grounds. Irène had gone there to interview some of a group of demonstrators who were walking back and forth with signs decrying the government's collusion with an array of business interests in manifold secret or unacknowledged controls of South American governments. Irène's English was fluent but, as a precaution against the (real, however slight) possibility of mistaking some part of her interlocutor's meaning, her habit was to tape-record the conversation rather than jotting down summaries or portions of it, and then to hear it again afterwards. In the conduct of an interview, then, her eyes were freed to wander as they pleased while the machine caught words. That morning while she spoke with the demonstrators her roving gaze had been arrested by the figure of a young woman (it was Mouse) dressed in squaw's buckskin and bone jewelry, with red and yellow warpaint on her cheeks and a feather in her black braided hair, standing near the fence some distance away.

She was very thin, it was a chilly morning, her interesting clothing wasn't warm enough. She should at least have worn something around her naked shoulders. She was hugging herself, her right hand over a copper ornament she wore on her left arm. From time to time she would break into a little shuffling dance—her floppy moccasins could hardly have warmed her feet much.

Some of the pedestrians hurrying along the windy sidewalk glanced at her without surprise or interest. Others stared, some laughed and pointed at her. Sometimes she watched with curiosity as if they were unusual and repellent zoo specimens. Then she would be lost in a brown study, looking at the concrete, until the cold brought her out of it into her soft shuffle-dance. And sometimes she would go to the curb and sight along the famous avenue. It was November, the red and yellow on her cheeks was strong rich warpaint.

When Irène had completed her interview she came over to the young woman and introduced herself, explaining that she was a journalist (true) compiling a chatty report of who happened to be there then (fabricated—Irène in her work often resorted to such ploys but rarely outside it, as now). She wanted to talk with the young woman, she went on to say, since her readers would like to know something about her. As she spoke Irène's pale eyes behind her large spectacles played one of their characteristic tricks, rolling far up to the right and then far up to the left, as if she were searching her memory for something that was about to come to her.

After a moment Mouse said, "I don't speak English." She said it in English in a way that prompted Irène to say, "But you speak French, then," in French.

Mouse did speak a very idiosyncratic French which Irène learned to understand soon, which more slowly she was beginning to speak. At its most familiar it was a Québecois, there were less familiar Portuguese components, and there were completely unfamiliar components, some from Oneida and others attributable to none of these nor to any other natural language, which Irène correctly took to be spontaneously generated products of the mix. At first, for six or eight weeks, listening to Mouse talk, Irène grew moderately proficient at assigning this or that peculiarity to this or that language, but she gave it up for idle. Idle or worse: Irène knew that for Mouse there were no discontinuities among the components. Mouse didn't jump from French to Portuguese to Oneida, she spoke her own language, one in which Irène could never be fluent: it resembled French in too many ways, so many she would never quite be able to hear it as it was, seamless. As it turned out, Mouse also spoke and understood rather more English than she had led Irène to believe when they first met. "But you speak French, then," Irène had said. "Aren't you cold?"

Instead of translating all she had first said she had simply introduced herself and the two of them had talked, had gone to Georgetown to stroll about the congenial streets there, had dined together slowly and very agreeably and then later had found themselves making love still more slowly and agreeably in an expensive hotel room, and then talking more, laughing, in one another's arms until they fell asleep.

Mouse had gone to Pennsylvania Avenue to participate in a demonstration of protest—not that covered by Irène but one of Native Americans protesting the U.S. government's abrogation of treaties with them. Unfortunately that demonstration had taken place two days before, Irène knew. Mouse had accepted the information with a breathtaking gloom—she had bought her buckskin squaw's clothes for the occasion, and Mouse was poor—that lasted five minutes and then vanished without leaving a trace.

The sidewalks of Georgetown were crowded with shoppers patronizing the interesting shops, children returning from school, busy idle young people, nineteen- and twenty-year-olds coming up out of a subterranean eatery with sandwiches to consume leaning against parked cars, street vendors of flowers, of handmade belts, candles, jewelry, of pretzels and of the various underground newspapers as well as circumspect vendors of hashish, lovemaking, and other proscribed goods, older women and men with their dogs, and many others passed before the crowded shop windows or clean pastel townhouses on the swept sidewalks under the naked trees.

Outside the unpretentious French restaurant Mouse suggested that perhaps she ought to remove her warpaint before dinner but Irène wouldn't hear of it and in fact the paint was not removed until the next morning when each of them noticed with a small shock that it had come barely mussed through the night. The restaurant was crowded and cozy, the staff accomplished, the food and drink good. There was no mockery of Mouse here, no gazing or whispering. Well-behaved eyes quietly took note, leading others to do the same a moment later. Some brows rose slightly, there were fleeting smiles and frowns among the candle flames and laughter, no more. The still more discreet eyes at the hotel, where people from several countries in native dress came and went in the lobby, where all was subdued and costly, seemed to note nothing at all.

Normally the hotel's unctuousness, following on the pleasure of the thronging streets and the happy dinner, would have weighed on Irène but tonight she was almost oblivious—captivated, swept off her feet, charmed by Mouse's dark acquiescence, her dark trust like that of a child in a stranger's care. It was as if all one did or said was alike strange to Mouse and all alike taken seriously, accepted gracefully without understanding or judgement, with goodwill. Irène had encountered nothing like it in her various brief romances or in the course of her long love of Jean-Luc.

They had been voluble during the afternoon and evening and at intervals through the night, but in the morning they were quiet. At breakfast they exchanged addresses and phone numbers, invitations and promises to meet again soon, small realistic promises. Irène had left Mouse on a street corner in the northwest. As she drove away she saw in the rearview mirror that Mouse alone on the pavement did not turn to watch the retreating car or to wave. Shaken and heady, twice between Washington and her house in the woods Irène narrowly escaped death. Jean-Luc had been grading student examination papers under the walnut tree. "Hi." "Hi."

Irène later learned that Mouse had expected never to see her again when they said good-bye first on the northwest street corner. What she had put out of her mind the afternoon and night before had then begun to occupy her bitterly: the belief that she had provided a momentary diversion, that letters she might write wouldn't be answered, that if she telephoned to ask for another meeting she would find Irène polite, busy, and carefully vague. Long hidden from Irène, Mouse's hopelessness had waned slowly with some painful resurgences through the good-byes that followed, in Washington at Mouse's apartment, at the house in the woods and elsewhere. At the second good-bye Mouse had given Irène the tiny clay pot she had brought from Amazonian Brazil that now sat on the kitchen table between Irène's hand and the toaster holding a wishbone, some weeds and a weedy feather.

Irène's eyes slid sideways in the other direction not to see anything but because she was listening to Mouse move upstairs.

Ho-hum, what to do now? A blaring waltz? Or maybe washing dishes without any music. Breaking some of the dishes maybe.

Chantal and Jean-Luc returned from the beach refreshed, with no stories to tell. They had walked, talked, worked, seen three old movies on television and two newer ones in almost empty theaters. There were apprehensive smiles on their faces. Little Chantal, who could be drab, had a bit of a glow on and Jean-Luc in jeans and a sweater, his large ears protruding through dark locks blown awry, was the rangy sailor everyone wants to love or be for a night ashore.

Their fears of a crazed ire proved groundless for once.

They said hello to Mouse and then ignored her except when it seemed she might serve as a meter for readings of Irène's mood. Irène herself was comically well behaved. With an air of graciously feigned interest she asked whether the car had given them any trouble. They were taken aback. "No," said Chantal in a way, a voice through whose assumed resignation some less dignified annoyance peeped. But that was it. Irène said, "Oh good," and went on to remark in an ordinary voice that such-and-such a person had telephoned. They would have felt foolish reading anything into the remark and yet since they couldn't trust Irène's pleasantness they were left feeling foolish anyway. Chantal went up to unpack. Jean-Luc delivered himself of habitual breezy laments about how many inept essays he had to correct before his first class in the morning. Mouse was amused.

She and Irène found ferns in the woods the next day and brought some back to the house and potted them. It was good because the frost came only a few days after that. The ferns grew on a certain hillside covered with pines. Mouse led the way—she had found the place before on one of her solitary walks. To reach the hillside of ferns they had to jump streams and cross some low marshy ground. As they went Mouse beat a pail with a trowel and sang loudly to apprise venomous snakes of their coming. Irène tried to help by singing too but she found that keeping pace with Mouse was all she had breath for. Back at the house they set the ferns in corners where the light was indirect, diffuse, and steady as it had been under the pines.

The following week Chantal moved all her things into the house and what had been the guest bedroom became hers. But it could still accommodate guests since Chantal slept with Jean-Luc in his bedroom, which earlier had been his and Irène's. Mouse's room, where she and Irène usually slept, had been a guest room before she came to live there. Irène had an office or study with a narrow bed in it where she sometimes slept. A guest could sleep there too on occasion.

The people Mouse would most have liked to provide shelter for, to cook for and to laugh and talk with, were too poor and lived too far away in other countries to come there, but guests did come to stay for weekends or weeks. Chantal's sister came from Montréal once and once a friend of Chantal's came down. All the other guests were friends of Irène's and Jean-Luc's, visitors from France, New York, California and other such places. Most of them had known Irène and Jean-Luc for a long time, most of them were meeting Mouse for the first time, none had met Chantal before. Some of them were kind and interesting, many were tediously affected and full of themselves. Almost all talked about books, newspapers, magazines, things they had read or written or were currently reading or writing or wanted to read or write. The few who had anything to say to Mouse beyond token hellos and good-byes were those who had known Irène longest, some since before she had met Jean-Luc. Even to these, whom she liked, Mouse said little—she had not read many books—but their stories and jokes, the way they laughed and played and mocked Irène made her feel happy and made her want them to stay longer and come oftener. Because they were too rare. Whoever was visiting, Chantal usually would be busy with her studies but Mouse often stayed on unobtrusively at the dinner table or in the living room. And what she observed of the general pattern of how things went with the stream of visitors seemed unfair. Why should most of it center and flow about Jean-Luc? Even when there were no guests he and Chantal and often Irène too acted as if naturally and necessarily at the center of the household, of its arrangements and decisions and fun, had to be Jean-Luc, the man, the only penis, the only moustache. Mouse complained of it to Irène.

"You're right," Irène said. "It's ridiculous. Chantal resents it too. She wanted to get another man to live here."

"Who though?"

"I know. Anyway I can't help seeing that as sort of an ass-backwards solution. It might do Jean-Luc good, especially if it was somebody who could turn little Chantal's head. But for us I think it would be avoidance more than solution. Because, Mouse, for us the real problem is the way we think, and it seems to me that what we ought to do is absolutely refuse to let another man live here, should the question arise—not that it's likely to—so we can have a chance to work it through without lowering the stakes, without any bleeding off or blurring. And you're as guilty as anybody. More than me. In fact of the four I'm the least guilty. You, Mouse, you pussyfoot around Jean-Luc as if he's your father or something.

"I mean, what the fuck difference should gender make as far as anything important is concerned? I don't even like the idea of 'sexual orientation.' Desiring people according to gender is like desiring according to skin color, and there may be equally pernicious side effects. But let that pass, for the moment. I'm willing to accept as a quirk or rather as a let's say morally neutral and perhaps basic characteristic of yours the fact that people of one whole gender get nowhere with you, that you've no inclination to make love with any of them. Well, or it's not quite that I 'accept' it—I don't 'accept' the fact that your hair is black or that, hmm, that you like to dance. Okay, I want your 'sexual orientation' to be like that for me, something I just know and take into account. Even though I may also hold that if fewer people had gender-specific sexual inclinations we'd have a less crazy and wearisome world. No contradiction. In fact the bias of your taste probably works like a drop of antidote in a toxic sea.

"But none of that's very important. What is, is that you discriminate according to gender in matters that have nothing to do with getting into people's beds or getting them into yours. And that I object to. I object to it in Chantal too in principle, though I can't muster much concern for the state of her soul. But you and I need to do better. You especially. Why pussyfoot? Why let it matter that he's a man rather than say a woman who doesn't happen to turn you on? You'd treat him differently if he were. Admit it, stop trying to kiss me. It's true, Mouse."

The frost came, leaves changed color and fell, the black walnuts in the tree in front of the house fell and the squirrels gathered some of them and Mouse gathered others during the long days when Jean-Luc and Chantal were in Charlottesville and Irène in Washington. Grey winter rains came and rotted the fallen leaves and walnut husks, the grass that had turned partly grey—rivers and streams ran opaque orange-red with clay then.

Grasshoppers died, industrious ants stocked and fortified their winter quarters. Many animals were going to sleep. There were dark flocks of birds in the grey sky, there were cardinals in the woods. Chantal and Irène and Jean-Luc and Mouse cut wood one clear Saturday, bundled up with wool caps and scarves and laughing. In the afternoon the icy rain recommenced. They built the first fire and drank mulled wine with orange peel floating in it. Almost every day it rained colder and colder. Beautiful crickets in the house sang more cheerily, as out of gratitude for shelter and warmth. Mouse listened to them when Irène was away in Washington and Chantal and Jean-Luc away in Charlottesville. She listened to the rain and the jet planes passing and to the cardinals.

She listened to records and tape recordings in the living room. Irène and Jean-Luc had an excellent sound system with strange speakers on pedestals in two corners of the room which worked according to principles no one understood, projecting the sound not forward toward the center of the room but backward. The sound was magnificent but not really verisimilar. The hearer seemed in the midst of the ensemble or, with solos, actually inside the played instrument or singer's throat. Mouse listened to her own tapes and records, Brazilian dances from the interior, Gilles Vigneault, Barbara. Sometimes she danced, clapped and sang with the recorded music, sometimes in an improvised costume. Sometimes she forgot the music, she grew so absorbed in creating her costume, using cosmetics or colored pencils, arranging and ornamenting her hair to become Columbine or Cleopatra or one of Cleopatra's slave-girls or a Jivaro or Ticuna warrior or medicine dancer. She would work faster and faster in front of the bathroom mirror, dash away for colored paper, jewelry, a feather, something for a spear or diadem, and then back to the mirror barefoot, heart pounding. Outside a car door slammed—Mouse flew down the hallway and peeked out. It was Irène. Mouse ran downstairs and hid behind a door. Irène found her blushing and stifling laughter with one hand over her mouth. Irène marvelled, Mouse struck poses, laughing at herself, ran upstairs and came back with a camera, made Irène photograph her. When it wasn't Irène, when it was Jean-Luc or someone else, Mouse locked herself in the bathroom until she had washed away her maquillage, undone her costume and coiffure. She strolled quietly back to her room with what she had used or worn hidden under a bath towel and then skipped down to hear another record.

Or alone in the house she might set the mechanism to play one side of a record, Vigneault, over and over all afternoon, all morning. Mouse would sit in an easy chair or in the lovely old wood and cane wheelchair, smoking cigarettes, listening and thinking. She tied her fine coarse long straight hair loosely back. This Mouse was skin and bones, absurdly beautiful, brown-skinned and distinct, her large eyes dark as possible, with long fingers, small brown and pink breasts, a dark thick bush or mat of pubic hair. She was an excellent mimic of others' characteristic gestures, stances and gaits. Hers were less accessible. Sometimes when a record was playing she went to the kitchen and prepared something small and savory—adding vinegar and thyme and olives to bland pig's feet out of a jar. The music sounded more real from in the kitchen. Mouse cleared the table and set a place for herself, with a folded paper napkin and a wineglass. She ate slowly. When she was done she washed only the dishes and utensils from that meal.

The living room sound system included a radio. On rare occasions Mouse listened to it, though never for long. The songs were too similar to be very interesting. So were the advertisements and announcements and other pieces of talk that more than the music made Mouse switch the radio off soon. She could disregard them longer on the cheap old portable radio in her room. Only Charlottesville stations came in clearly during the cold days of rain when she was alone and therefore free to fill the house with sound when she pleased—Washington was too distant—and the little town delivered its football game scores and bustling shopping centers through the pedestalled speakers too fulsomely for Mouse's liking, in a language whose distastefulness they intensified.

Mouse's aversion to English was longstanding. The queasy fat sound of it had always offended her, its way of moving like a dirty cripple. And the more she'd seen of what it let its users do with and to it, each other, people who didn't use it, indeed much of the world, the more she shrank from it. She spoke it seldom and badly, ludicrously she knew. Yet in the mouths of those who supposedly made best use of it it sounded if anything worse to her. She would turn off the radio then and hear another record or not. But none of the recorded music satisfied her so much as the remembered Oneida and Seneca songs her Oneida grandmother had sung her for lullabys when she was a child.

The tongue-and-groove boards of Mouse's room were baroquely hung with artifacts she had bought or been given and natural treasures she had found in the Virginia woods or on the banks of the Amazon, with many pictures—drawings and photographs, watercolors she had made, picture postcards, reproductions of photos cut from magazines and travel brochures. It was a small room at the front with a flower box in the window. Her furniture came from a Washington Goodwill store. The oriental rug was Irène's and Jean-Luc's.

Monticello, designed and inhabited by an early president of the U.S. said to have been distinguished for the range of his talents and comparative probity, may be seen on some U.S. nickels and is situated on a hill near Charlottesville, Virginia. Mouse, Jean-Luc, Irène and Chantal drove there one cold overcast Saturday to tour the buildings and grounds. It seemed that the smiling women who led small groups from room to room, who provided bits of information, humorous anecdotes and answers for questions asked, were descendants of the Mr. Jefferson. Printed summaries in French of what they said in English were available at no extra charge. The erstwhile president had designed an ingenious mechanism for a pair of paned-glass doors such that it was necessary to push only one of them open for its fellow to open automatically. The system still operated and its secret—toothed wheels and a chain under the floor that transmitted applied force from the axle of one door to that of the other—had but recently been discovered during restoration operations. To guard against theft of his books the man had supplemented the customary bookplates with a clever system of unobtrusive ciphers inscribed on certain pages. There was an artificial pool in which edible fish could be kept conveniently alive nearby. Under the house ran a tunnel off which lay wine, cider, and rum cellars, the kitchen and a small museum where perfume flasks and underclothing were displayed. There was also an "air tunnel," a narrow conduit enclosing an arrangement of pulleys whereby chamber pots could leave the house and reappear some distance down the hill at a point screened from view by shrubbery planted for the purpose and then, emptied and well washed, return underground to the house. This device would have been more admirable had it emptied and cleaned the pots itself. Nor were living quarters for those who had done such work to be seen. In the parking lot Mouse noticed license plates from more than ten U.S. states and three outside nations. Mouse herself didn't know how to drive a car. She was afraid to learn.

She had very little money. When she came to live with Irène and Jean-Luc she had used meager savings to pay her third of the rent, food, electricity and phone bills. Ostensibly she still paid her share—a quarter now, with Chantal there—but it was with money Irène gave her, not quite secretly yet not so as to attract Jean-Luc's and Chantal's notice. Irène gave her the money gracefully and with no nonsense. She had said, "If sometime you have an income and I don't, you'll support me." Irène was right. And it seemed impossible for Mouse to earn any money while she lived there. Why then should it matter if Chantal and Jean-Luc knew of the arrangement?

A few times Mouse rode to Washington with Irène and was disheartened. If she stayed with Irène she was in the way. Her efforts to help with Irène's work never succeeded, always more or less hampered and sometimes annoyed. It was as bad when she tried simply to be unobtrusive. They might then separate and meet later. But being alone and aimless in the cold in the ugly grey city, suffering the ugly cajolery and threatening of its derelict men, buying a magazine, a lunch, a record without being able to think of any other way to pass the time was no damn good at all.

Irène drove up to Washington almost every day. Tuesdays and Thursdays Jean-Luc and Chantal drove down to Charlottesville together in one car and on the other weekdays they drove separately. Sometimes they all came back for dinner, sometimes only one or two, occasionally none. Weekends all four might visit Monticello, say, or cut wood together. More often everyone was busy, especially Chantal, reading and writing hidden away in this or that room, or Mouse and Irène were together in either's room or in the kitchen, Jean-Luc and Chantal were together elsewhere in the house or had driven away together. Mouse tried to be happy. She was happy when they all cut firewood together, each helping each, each making the others laugh outside in the cold and then inside before the first fire with mulled wine. She was when she and Irène were alone together, except when Irène was bitterly crazy, harsh and unkind. And when Mouse was alone at the house almost anything might make her feel happy. Once she saw a skunk family cross the porch. They came up the steps at one side, crossed, descended at the other side and continued on their way. It was late afternoon, the rain had cleared and was freezing on the ground. Once for an hour Mouse played with a squirrel. He sat on a branch of the walnut tree, she stood some twenty meters off. If she stepped forward he would scold until he had halted her advance or made her retreat. Then he would watch to see what she was up to next. If she scolded him he tilted his head and listened.

But there were bleak mornings and hasty dinners when mere truce seemed to obtain in the household. Worse, in the twinkling of an eye the spirit could change, Irène treat Chantal like an enemy, Jean-Luc cease to acknowledge Mouse's existence, he close his heart to Irène and she harry him without mercy. Then it seemed to Mouse that someone must have cursed her to make her love Irène and be trapped there. The hopeless strife broke out one Saturday morning and made an excursion they had planned impossible. Chantal and Jean-Luc had driven somewhere to escape. Irène had impassively watched them go and then she had gone up to her study. She was typing. Mouse had been speechless and nearly paralyzed. She sat down on a chair in the kitchen. She, Irène, Jean-Luc, and Chantal seemed utterly shameful to her. A malevolence seemed at work among them, they were powerless against it, it would sniff out the smallest good or happiness and crush it. Mouse put her hands over her face and began to sob. Irène came for a cup of coffee and found her. Irène held her and kissed her and said good comforting soothing things full of love. But Mouse was not comforted or soothed at all, and Irène's good love was frightening because it seemed that it too would be sniffed out and destroyed. Why not?

A year or so before when Mouse first moved into the house there had been terrible times with Irène. Mouse had said, "Do you think it would be okay for me to come and live with you? Sometimes when you're not busy we can play.

When you're too sad I can kiss you, you can rest your head in my lap. Can you spare a little corner for me?" Mouse meant a little corner in Irène's day-to-day life but in the beginning Irène had seemed to think she meant only a corner of the house. Mouse had protested. It was hard enough to bear when Irène was spending lots of time working and when she was spending most of the remainder not even with Jean-Luc but rather flirting and talking folly with some house guest Mouse had to protest, and always then Irène had gone into rages and yelled that Mouse shouldn't presume to *rule* her, that they weren't *married,* that she would not allow Mouse to be her *warden,* pacing, seeming to find what she was to say inscribed on the ceiling and emphasizing the crucial words—*warden, married, rule*—with a very characteristic sort of indignant curtsey, a sweeping step backwards, sweeping her arms open, palms turning out and up, with an inclination of the head so that the gesture ended with her staring at Mouse's feet. Jean-Luc intimidated Irène too much for her ever to abandon herself to such theatrical anger against him or even before him—it happened when Mouse and Irène were alone there. Irène worked herself up (Mouse could see). Her rage quickly became its own fuel and when that happened nothing Mouse did would calm it. Mouse could see that then the one thing that mattered about her was that she was the object of the rage, Mouse and no one else. There was no good way out then: the episode could only end with a crueller word, slammed doors. Or, as happened one night, still more dramatically. They were standing face-to-face in the middle of the kitchen. Irène had taken Mouse by the shoulders and shaken her, yelling something about something. She had released Mouse and seemed to wait for a reply that didn't come. Irène stood with her feet apart, her arms open and slightly bent. Mouse opened her mouth and inhaled. Irène brought her arm up and gave Mouse a full hard slap with her open palm. She had retraced the arc and delivered a second blow with the back of her hand to the other side of Mouse's face. The second blow made blood pour out of Mouse's nose and tears out of her eyes and maybe therefore had been the last. Mouse at the time, tears and blood smeared on her face, in her mouth, on her hands and clothes and dripping on the linoleum in the kitchen and in the bathroom as Irène bathed her and stanched the bleeding with ice, had been able to notice only that the rage had given way to tenderness. But she soon saw that Irène had shocked and appalled herself.

There hadn't been any more blows nor after the first four months had Irène abandoned herself to theatrical anger. Mouse had found less to protest about or complain of. They had come to understandings of each other and were confident.

With Jean-Luc, Mouse hadn't fared so well. He had been shy and playful with her in the beginning and had sanctioned, even encouraged her and Irène in their love. Mouse had wondered at him, almost fallen in love with him too. She had bought or made little gifts and would have done almost anything he asked. He asked almost nothing. He had behaved similarly, Mouse learned, during earlier affairs of Irène's. If after several months Irène and Mouse had stopped making love, stopped being in love with each other, if Mouse hadn't wanted to move into the house, if Irène hadn't wanted her to, Jean-Luc would certainly now be greeting Mouse with the courtly proprietariness she had seen prior lovers of Irène's elicit. When Mouse first came to live there, during the first four or five months, she told herself that Jean-Luc's increasing reserve was the product of her own over-anxious imagination or, insofar as real, it was understandable, involuntary and short-term. After two years Mouse still thought it partly involuntary but she had stopped trying to understand it. She had stopped trying to propitiate him.

Mouse tried to be strong and happy and optimistic. Usually she succeeded. When the cold grey rain was blowing she sloshed out through the mud and saw cardinals flash from tree to tree. When Irène's work kept her overnight in Washington she telephoned to explain and Mouse wasn't troubled by jealous suspicions. What Irène said was true and even if it weren't, even if she had run into an old friend or lover or had let a stranger pick her up, that wasn't so bad either because she would be back tomorrow. Mouse found some cheese and good bread and wine in the kitchen. Apparently Chantal and Jean-Luc wouldn't be home tonight either—Chantal hadn't yet found anyone to move into her apartment, she and he sometimes slept there. Tonight only Mouse would be home. She turned off the sound system and all the lights downstairs. Upstairs she turned off the lights in the corridor and in her room, all the electric lights. She lit a candle in her room and lit a cigarette from the candle's flame. What if she fell asleep and set the house on fire? She had never before been the only one there overnight. There were noises that were a little scary.

Mouse turned on her portable radio. Sweeping the dial

slowly across music and talk, she seemed to cross a ghost of Portuguese. She smiled. Rapid talk distorted and filtered through interferences might seem to be in any language whatsoever and the illusion was astoundingly tenacious once the ear had made its decision. And then once the language was suddenly heard aright the illusion was irretrievable, unimaginable even. The process delighted Mouse whenever it happened. She nursed the dial back toward the faint pulsing station. It wasn't . . . it wasn't Portuguese . . . Spanish, wasn't it Spanish? Yes, and then music, out of phase with the pulses, it was "La Bamba," then talk, it was . . . it was from Cuba, from Havana. . . . Mouse listened for a long time to pulses of music and talk. She listened and understood some of the Spanish as the interference increased until the pulses were no longer discernible in the shush and whine. She clicked off the radio. She listened and began to be frightened. The house was weirdly still and outside in the night there was no sound at all. What had happened? Mouse was afraid to open her curtains. She opened them and looked out. Snow was falling, the ground was already covered. Mouse blew out her candle, wrapped a blanket around her and sat in the window. She wondered whether Jean-Luc and Chantal and Irène would be able to get back. The snow kept falling. Mouse's knowledge of world history was scant. She had not studied it at a university or a college. She had not studied anything at such a place. Mouse had no credentials for her knowledge.

CHANTAL'S DILIGENCE paid off. She ended her first semester of graduate study with a perfect 4.0 grade point average and in April, her midterms past, the second semester boded as fair. Beyond this proof of not having failed, she was aware of less coarsely quantitative indices of success. The word was, apparently, that she was someone to watch. In January one professor—not Jean-Luc—had announced in a confidential evaluation written for her dossier that she was "perhaps more promising than any other student I recall having encountered in the last five years, and with a very pleasant classroom presence if a trifle solemn." Second and third year graduate students she met knew of her and showed a certain deference. When she was introduced to professors they nodded and smiled, "Oh yes. . . ." It was as though by some consensus reached with astonishing dispatch the course of most of the rest of her life had been decided, and congratulatory telegrams were starting to arrive. Almost as she had predicted, being a native speaker of French had given her but a slight edge and that indirectly: she happened to be well versed in a particular French way of talking and writing about literary texts that was becoming fashionable at the university in Charlottesville just then. Other factors—chance, native shrewdness and of course diligence—contributed more directly to the payoff. Her face, body, and manner hadn't counted either way much, never mind what Jean-Luc said about his colleagues' obscene imaginings. Had his smoothed his way here? Chantal wondered. Certainly not altogether verifiably, yet Chantal found it impossible to believe that his mere physical charm, his beauty hadn't sometimes been the fleeting subliminal nothing at the crux that made all the difference, determined the whole outcome of an interplay of hard-nosed pragmatic considerations. And Chantal also opined that Jean-Luc himself was savvy. Never mind how he fumbled and puffed his pipe and lost track of things. In April Chantal knew better.

She stood on a brick walk beside one of the serpentine walls in the university grounds Friday afternoon early. The springy weather was pleasant enough. Chantal glanced down the hill, a long tidy expanse of new grass and lovely trees. She snapped open her shoulder bag and withdrew an appointment book, flipped it open to today. At three she was to meet Jean-Luc's and Irène's friend M. Queille at the airport, and before then she had to find a birthday present for Mouse.

The tight-assed professors Jean-Luc had said dreamed of Chantal interested her little. No more did the students who noticed her more than Jean-Luc cared to admit. The students—she watched them salute one another on the walks and was unmoved by their cheer. They were male and of northern European, British, ancestry, with the rarest exceptions. Many wore the same kind of modified moccasin and scrubbed valor. Who were they? Precisely how did they understand, in what mood accept and sanction their rulers' meddling with the world's life? What had happened to their eyes? Even here much glared through the tidiness, enormities glared. Chantal was giddy. The lawn swept far down to a low stone wall with sitting students. Over the wall lay a street with two-way traffic, cars and bicycles, people crossing. Above the street was a sidewalk on which at this hour numerous people stood or walked. Behind them up from the pavement's edge stood a variegated little facade of restaurant, clothier, bookstore behind which the blue sky swept all the way up. *Oh really?* thought Chantal.

Flip, snap. Proceed. Chantal felt peculiarly unqualified for finding something to give Mouse but by two forty-five she had accomplished that chore and sat in the airport glancing over a newspaper and sipping black coffee from a styrofoam cup. The plane was on time. Chantal recognized M. Queille from Jean-Luc's description, introduced herself and explained that neither Jean-Luc nor Irène had been able to meet his plane. Chantal proceeded. "How was your flight?"

"I prefer trains. Are you one of Jean-Luc's students?"

"Hmm. I took a couple of his classes in the summer. Does that mean I am or only was a student of his? He and Irène and another woman and I live at the same place."

"Splendid."

"I think they said you'd never been there."

"That's the case whatever they said. Look, Chantal. I've brought along someone who's working on a project with me. Will there be room? If not you should drop us at a hotel. I didn't have time to phone—or rather I did, but no answer."

"No, there's room. But where . . . ?"

"Here. Claude, Chantal. Chantal, Claude."

After saying "Hello" with a friendly smile, Claude settled herself into the back seat and remained silent. M. Queille—Gaétan—and Chantal conversed. She rather liked his fuzzy hair, his silly clothes and the way he turned toward and away from her as they talked. She liked his combination of fatigue and good-humored liveliness. He explained that for several years he had been in an Amsterdam communications collective which served as a clearing-house for research into aspects of the visual environment, especially manmade visual environments, and which also carried out its own projects, one of which he and Claude had just completed (except for format work to be done back in Holland), a documentation of southern California vernacular architecture in slides and videotape.

Chantal said, "I've never seen the West Coast. I know I ought to."

"By all means."

"Would I like it?"

"Moot, superfluous. Good heavens child, it's there and it won't change to please you. You talk as if you were contemplating a purchase!"

"Of a plane ticket, yes—or a rail ticket, or gasoline."

"Yes but still, you know? Though your case is hardly uncommon I'm still capable of genuine bewilderment at it. 'We liked Yugoslavia better than Greece.' 'Capetown left us with mixed feelings.' Viewed objectively, these are lunatic sentences and yet you know as well as I how at large they are. If what you want is to 'like' California, Chantal, if and when you go there to have a look at it you could probably find a drug to guarantee that you like it."

"Why bother to go someplace one's not going to like,

though. When there are lots of other places that wouldn't necessitate drugs."

"Are there? I suppose it would depend on the traveller. . . . Well, perhaps you're right, Chantal. I see I can't intimidate you into abandoning your position anyway. Perhaps you're wise and we should only go to places reasonably sure to please us, should arrange so as to view only what we're confident of liking, should entertain only comforting notions."

"'Should'?" said Chantal. "Perhaps we do!"

Gaétan smiled. "There's also the matter of closure in common formats or gestalts. You've seen the East Coast, I take it, and also this locale and maybe other parts. So if you don't then see California it's bound to look like an omission and to demand explanation. Rather than spend the rest of your life explaining how it could be you didn't see California, it might be easier to go there."

"Easier still simply to avow having gone when the question arises. Fictional closure."

"Good, except that those who've made that closure in reality will want to line their impressions up against yours, and those who haven't nor pretend to have essayed the figure will, as you did, ask whether they're going to like California or, in idle curiosity, whether they would like it were they there instead of where they are. In either case you find yourself having to support your first fiction with much more detailed ones. In which discrepancies are likely to crop up, you know."

"No, I think instead I'll say I have nothing to say about California, that I have absolutely no memory of it. They'll imagine I want to avoid the subject for private, personal reasons. A painful event, probably the end of an affair, indissolubly linked with all my memories of the place. They won't pry. I'll quickly shun the inconsiderate ones who do." Chantal glanced into the rearview mirror. Claude seemed lost in thought, not listening to the front-seat conversation nor watching the flow of terrain outside the car. After a moment Chantal said, "More than two hundred millionaires reside in the county around Charlottesville. The county board of supervisors determines the tax rate. The real estate tax rate for this fiscal year was set at about six dollars for each one hundred of assessed value, which is about fifteen percent of appraised value. Appraised value is officially defined as a certain fraction of market value. This year the estimated total appraised taxable property value for the county was ninety-four million dollars."

"Good heavens." Gaétan peered out his window.

"No," said Chantal. "We're in a different county now. Though some fabulously wealthy people live here too."

Gaétan yawned, rumpled his fuzzy hair. Claude watched flakes of dandruff falling to his shoulders. He rubbed his eyes with the back of a fist and yawned again. "Are you a Marxist, Chantaaanhh . . . ?"

"Isn't everyone?"

"Have you read Marx?"

"I have, in fact. The first volume of *Capital*."

"Like it?" He was gazing innocently at his fingernails. Chantal laughed. For a while as she drove in silence she was remembering the tears Marx's stern childlike sarcasm and ironies had once filled her eyes with as she read.

Gaétan said, "Lenin?"

"Mmm . . . some."

"Trotsky? Luxemburg?"
"No. By the way, Gaétan: this list . . ."
"Yes?" He nodded, starting to smile.
"Does the figure permit closure?"
"Good heavens, my dear—am I likely to know?"

During the last lap of the journey, the long gravel drive in poor repair, Gaétan thought Chantal might be at least slightly reckless as a driver, the little automobile hopped about so.

Jean-Luc didn't know how to find Mouse a birthday gift either. Two years ago when Irène informed him that Mouse wanted to come and live with them, he had not asked for time to think although the proposal took him by surprise. "Okay," he had said, "it might work. But it might not, so you have to grant me the right to get the hell out if it proves unbearable for me."

"One always has that right," Irène had said, eminently reasonable. Yet there had been something preemptive about her gaiety and assurance. For that matter almost everything Irène did was in some way preemptive.

It proved unbearable often but Jean-Luc hadn't gotten the hell out. He had kept faith and dug in. The first winter and spring had been hardest, when on leave of absence from the university he was struggling to get a book on Molière (of all people) done. Mouse's mere presence changed Irène almost beyond recognition. The book didn't get done, it still wasn't done.

Before, when Mouse was coming for weekends, he had

thought her rather charming. He had thought her good for Irène, a relief from the increasing rigors of her work, an antidote he himself hadn't much provided for some time. Weekends Mouse and Irène had played and laughed like schoolgirls and during the week Irène had laughed with him too, been happier and less pontifical. He and Irène had done something they hadn't done for a couple of years—they had made love with each other.

The pattern might have persisted when Mouse moved in but it hadn't, Jean-Luc didn't know why. He had thought they were in a hiatus and then he had come to see that the pattern wasn't going to resume, it itself had been a hiatus. Jean-Luc became depressed and lethargic. Week after week when he should have been working he sat somewhere like a prisoner on death row. Nights he lay in bed, smoked, heard Irène and Mouse down the hall in Mouse's room making love or talking, and envisioned the ever bleaker indefinite extension of that life.

It was terrible and Irène's insensitivity, her complete failure to guess that gloom and resentment underlay his difficult cheer had aggravated the gloom and resentment until they would rush through. The silence he'd fallen into would break and accusations rush out angrily. When it happened Irène had been genuinely astounded. She had responded with conciliatory apologies at first and later and more characteristically with countercharges. "I can't know what's in your mind, Jean-Luc. You never ask me to do anything with you, you act as if you're glad to have me out of the way. Shit, it's unethical to complain now about months past, you don't have a leg to stand on. Don't make me laugh, nor make me crazy, don't do this to me." Jean-Luc had vetoed celebration of his birthday—it would have been a travesty. All the same Irène had slipped into his room and presented him with a very beautiful pocket watch. "In gratitude at the conclusion of my services?" he had asked. They had laughed and there had been other momentary lightenings of the gloom. It hadn't been easy to understand. Jean-Luc hadn't understood it.

Most of his life he had been a solitary sort, inclined to avail himself of long tracts of time in country houses or wherever with no one else. While Irène accused him of egocentricity, the matter was more complex since he was also more sociable than she, never wanted to leave parties so soon as she. Whatever the moral weight, though, Jean-Luc had always been content to be alone. But during the first months when Mouse and Irène were continually together Jean-Luc's very solitude soured. He felt unattractive, middle-aged, flabby. He felt as if he deserved to be alone.

Awash in depression he hung on though. Certainly it never entered his mind to "solve" the problem by leaving Irène. For better or worse he loved her so that copping out was unimaginable.

Things improved. A brief affair with a colleague's wife, a freckled woman he didn't find overwhelmingly attractive, helped. In her interminable sincerities occasional good sense could be counted on. Irène, at first solicitous and patronizing, soon took an aversion to the woman and made Jean-Luc promise not to bring her into the house for four or five days at a time. Jean-Luc tried to comply. Since the woman's husband pleasantly and adamantly refused to let her and Jean-Luc spend nights at her house, they sometimes went to motels but the attendant disadvantages would lead him to overlook Irène's injunctions and bring his lover to the house in the woods late at night. Then there were scenes, Irène with anything wrapped around her storming down from Mouse's bedroom to bar the door like a long-suffering wife in a melodrama.

Less from Irène's strictures than inertia Jean-Luc's and the freckled wife's dealings lapsed into attenuated friendliness, hellos at French department dinners, satisfaction. The woman's little daughter missed having Jean-Luc to play with. Jean-Luc's interest in his book revived some. Irène's and Mouse's inseparability was less at issue. Jean-Luc felt handsomer. He laughed more, girls in supermarkets flirted shamelessly with him and he loved it. Mouse had never seen an opera—one night Jean-Luc and Irène and she drove to Washington for *Tosca* and supper. The evening would have pleased Jean-Luc more if Mouse had spent it in Brazil; even so he enjoyed the outing and acquitted himself well. Then and at other times he rather wished he could be a woman and participate unconstrainedly in Irène's and Mouse's play. His recourse was avuncular expansiveness, warm enough and mildly ridiculous in itself and for the eager gratitude it elicited from Mouse. Perhaps she supposed that if she could turn him into a sweet crotchety old fart Irène would be all hers. Irène wouldn't ever be all hers.

Indeed, when he remembered to, Jean-Luc felt an abstract pity for the girl. There were signs that the outlandishly prolonged honeymoon was phasing out. There were quarrels, one night he had come home late to find Irène applying ice to stanch a bloody nose she had given Mouse. In these matters Irène was slow and cautious, but when she had come to a change of heart she was unrelenting. And Mouse didn't seem very well equipped for abandonment. On the other hand. . . . Once Jean-Luc had asked Irène what sorts of things she and Mouse found to talk about. The question had made Irène too indignant to answer.

Jean-Luc's students adored him, his colleagues enjoyed his company and when Chantal fell in love with him he thought it would be frivolous to complain of his lot. He certainly seemed luckier than many of the people he knew, and reading newspapers made him ashamed of niggling with questions of love and jealousy. He was well fed, clothed and housed, and war zones were so far away he had never seen a casualty in the flesh. Natural disasters—earthquakes, floods, epidemics and so forth—took place elsewhere.

Jean-Luc was uncommonly affectionate for one so well read and travelled and in other circumstances his affection would have gone out to Mouse. He was warm—were Mouse and Irène not lovers, were Mouse a chance acquaintance of Irène's and his, nothing was clearer than that he would have taken to Mouse whereas Irène would have appraised her at a first meeting, thereafter would scarcely have noticed her and would have frowned on Jean-Luc's squandering time in such a person's company. But as things were, toward Mouse his nature was baffled. How much easier things would have been had he felt affection for her! But he felt none and couldn't imagine anything that would ever let him feel any. The best Jean-Luc could feel toward Mouse was a blankness—as if she were a quite *ad hoc* and characterless minor character in a drama, a confidante in a tragedy, say. And sometimes it seemed that Irène had contrived this effect out of an instinctive didacticism, had baffled his natural affection to make him learn things she knew, coldnesses. But that was silly.

Things improved greatly during the summer when he and Chantal started being lovers. It had been a matter of principle with him to avoid amorous liaisons with students who were or might be in his classes. "With someone over whom you have that sort of power? Inexcusable," he had said. He had always kept the light flirtatiousness of his teaching style undirected in the classroom and outside it too, and not allowed himself even to entertain the possibility of further developments until after he had sent final grades and evaluations off to the registrar's office. "I was wondering," Irène had said with a poker face when with Chantal for the first time he became the lover of a current student, "I was wondering whether you've compromised yourself or simply changed your principles." Neither quite. It was more that this case seemed an exception. There was simply nothing problematic about Chantal's being his student. It was irrelevant. Things might have been more ticklish had she been less outstanding—Jean-Luc didn't know.

They made love more frequently than he and Irène had ever done, and he felt happier and more released doing it. When he was younger Jean-Luc had supposed that he knew basically everything there was to know about making love. Now with Chantal it was beginning to seem that he must never have known much since there wasn't much one could know. He had to smile. Making love was something one did without accumulating knowledge about it. Yet one certainly saw the difference between things going right or wrong, working or not. Yet even when it was bad it was good.

Jean-Luc and Chantal also conversed oftener and longer than he and Irène had done in years, since he first knew Irène. It pleased him. It didn't entirely satisfy him though. Something Chantal was saying sometimes with a shock reminded him of their ages and for the space of a heartbeat made the difference seem larger than it was. Jean-Luc didn't yet know what to make of these dizzying moments. He suspected that Chantal suffered analogous shocks and he intended to broach the subject. He never felt those shocks when he and Chantal were making love, almost never. Disconcerting moments there were occasioned more physiologically. They had been fucking pretty strenuously, had done and lain apart in torpor. A slow shock—that Chantal's flesh was just now repellent to him and that it was okay—had come and gone. Evidently she was dozing. He sat up and then kneeled, leaning and reaching over her for cigarettes on the night table. His cock dangled against her nipples. She opened her eyes. It was a quick fine shock to look into them and see that she and he were about to make love again.

Jean-Luc had grown from a beautiful innocent happy child to an adult extraordinarily free of pettiness, of wishes to hurt others, profoundly liberal, gentle and humane. In his innocence and harmlessness and strength he grew up to find late that there were such things as authority, reductiveness and violence at work in the world. Sometimes people thought him disingenuous but they were mistaken. He made extravagant expenditures of time and imagination for his friends' benefit and pleasure. Sometimes he felt

very tired, feared that maybe the reductivists were right—
or, if not that, that maybe he was going to have to give in to
them, be ground down to attributing bad motives to everyone and really espouse the cynicism he often played at for
fun. Even that fun seemed a little ignoble. He and Irène in
the beginning had played—she had made him laugh with
joy. But her spirit was not so kindred as had first seemed
the case. It had to be admitted that over the years Irène's
lack of innocence, her driven hardness had been inimical,
had killed or cut back some of what was best in him, his joy.
But with Chantal it burgeoned.

Then Irène had seemed to go intermittently psychotic.
Ouf, that was unpleasant and most because it made her
look monstrous to him. Sleeping beside Chantal he had
nightmares in which Irène was berserk—murderous. Jean-
Luc hid his anxiety. He could think of no way to help her.
He shielded Chantal when he could and hung on. Against
his will at this time the idea of leaving Irène would flash
across his mind. He tried not to notice. Fortunately soon
after Irène's wild assault on Chantal's tires her craziness
had seemed to undergo a spontaneous remission of sorts.
Jean-Luc was grateful.

Things were pretty good now except that Jean-Luc still
hadn't been able to bully himself into getting down to work
on the study he ought by now to have done half of. For that
he kept a little compartment of gloom at the back of his
mind. Irène had once said that he was the longer on intellect, she on will. His daily not beginning even the least con-
sequential preliminary skirmishing with Molière did seem
evidence of a shortage of will. As for intellect, what kind of
evidence was his almost daily—whenever his spirits were

high—believing he really would at last, or might well, start working on the book tomorrow?

It was a thorn and an albatross but it could be borne for now. Meantime there were always small tasks and chores and exasperations. One had to come up with a birthday gift for Mouse. Jean-Luc had to smile.

"By the way, where'd you meet him?"

"Louie? At The Candy Store, it's a bar opposite the crêperie. He's funny, Irène. Nice."

A mile south of the house Mouse and Irène sat on an outcrop of granite above a narrow deep gorge cut by an old stream that meanders through the woods there. Air cooled against the shaded ground spilled past them into the cleft onto the cold water. Clear sunlight fell over them and the rock. Irène had finished her work in Washington early and driven back, she and Mouse had come walking.

"Was getting off these two extra days a grief?" Irène asked.

"Not very. Boss man knows I might quit any day at all just if I've had a bad dream, so I think he's a little bit queasy to fire me. More, because by now people in the regular clientele ask for me to serve them."

Irène nodded. "And join them for a drink after work at this Candy Store. And then when that closes to go home with them for a nightcap. Meanwhile happening to make more or less passing reference to, what would it be?—travel, I should think, needing to get away from Washington soon for a couple of weeks with the right companion, somebody new. The Bahamas maybe, Rio would be fun. Or Spain for a lark, no? Or those with only their charming youth to dangle."

"Are the offers ever dangled in good faith?"

"Youth yes."

"But the trips?"

"Certainly not always. But sometimes, why not. And it shouldn't be hard to know when. Those who don't mean it want you to think they do, those who do mean it want you to know. But why am I telling you, Mouse? I'm sure you recognize genuine bait perfectly."

Neither woman looked at the other. Irène fingered a lock of her hair, she raised her eyebrows slightly as though she had asked a mischievous question. Mouse doodled on the stone with a twig. She sat listening to the birdsongs, her chin in the crook of an arm atop a knee. She wrote something on the stone and then reversed the twig to erase it. "So," she said. "It follows I'm loyal and faithful since you never see me disappear into the clouds a fortnight. Also you call me a liar."

"How?"

"Guess."

"No idea in the world."

"Here's a clue: I . . ."

"Stop it, Mouse—I don't feel like it. Good heavens, tell me what you meant or don't tell me, life is too short! Sometimes you . . ." Irène broke off, shaking her head. She inhaled. Her jaw tightened, her glance seemed to slip sideways and stop.

Mouse watched. No . . . , no, Irène had decided to wait obstinately for Mouse to speak. Mouse doodled for a moment with her twig pencil and then shrugged. She looked up and said, "Anyway, my dear Irène, you have the wrong picture of The Candy Store. It's no smart club where people think about delightful vacations or world travel. There's a photo of some Harlem Globetrotters over the bar, but not autographed. I think few of those there ever went outside Washington. Probably there's a fair percentage of Washington they haven't ventured into. They're largely black people, you see. Louie is black but he's only been in D.C. several months. He was a new face in the bar. I was one too of course. Louie's approximately fifty (he doesn't have a birth certificate).

"It was funny when I went in there the first time. I wanted to buy cigarettes before work. Everybody was black! You should have been a fly on the wall to watch, Irène, it was so funny. I wondered if they supposed I was one of them.

"So a silly guy in his cups started saying too many things to me and then . . ."

Irène interrupted. "What things?"

"I didn't try to listen. Well then I was championed. It was Louie. He told the guy, 'Buzz off, little weenie.' Louie isn't very tall, you'd have laughed to see it. The guy changed his manner completely. Then Louie offered me a drink. Oh sure he was flirting. I told him I was altogether a lady's girl, he said he didn't believe me. We had a good time talking and laughing."

"Ah, Mouse, you'd like to live in that bar, I think. Too bad. Louie's riding down with . . ."

"Ninon, yes. Boss man let her off tomorrow night too, it's incredible. Irène? Who is it that's coming for the weekend?"

"It's Gaétan. You remember the story I told you about

finding balloons hidden everywhere in my room and thanking Jean-Luc when it was really somebody else? That was Gaétan. We've known him forever. He toyed with several professions and finally a while ago he settled in some sort of communications group in Amsterdam. We haven't seen him in four or five years. He's frivolous and bright, I don't know. He'll like you. You may like him, he may bore you. He bores me sometimes. He and Jean-Luc used to start talking after dinner and not stop till noon the next day. I usually fell asleep."

"That goes without saying."

Irène was famous for leaving parties and conversations early. At parties she and Jean-Luc gave she might sneak upstairs at eleven or midnight and go to sleep without a word to anyone. The next morning she would explain that she had intended only to rest for ten minutes, nobody believed her and she knew it.

The two women smiled at each other. Irène moved closer and lay on her back with her head pillowed in Mouse's lap. Her hand encircled Mouse's ankle lightly. She relaxed. Since there was nothing behind Mouse to lean against she sat with straight arms angled behind, her palms on the stone. Mouse often settled into positions that looked uncomfortable and held them with no apparent strain for many times the time Irène or almost anyone else could have done.

There must once have been a little bridge across the crevice just here (though nothing of it remained) because the old path they had followed continued discernibly on the other side. It wasn't far—in fact it should be possible to leap across with a running start. It would be scary though.

Moss and stone were in the air, birds sang courting songs. Mouse said, "How is he for politics, Gaétan?"

Irène's eyes went coolly over Mouse, then away. She frowned. "Oh, Mouse, he. . . . How is anybody? Gaétan's the same. He doesn't advocate maintenance of coercion, privilege and inequality. He sings no paeans to the rule of almost all by almost none. He finds no excellence in mass murder *per se*, he doesn't foment mediocrity. You won't find Gaétan in a kiosk in a park or a television set urging us not to consider assuming control of our lives. I feel sure that a graph of all votes he has cast in his adult life would show him fairly consistently supporting the lesser or least evil offered. What's to say? Gaétan's judicious and pathetic, grist for the mill just like everybody. He's rather like Jean-Luc that way. I love him and I like him very much. Even when he's insufferable."

"Did you ever make love with him?"

"I don't think so."

"Would it be good if he lived with us?"

Irène gave a voiceless laugh through her nose. She looked at her hand, white encircling Mouse's brown ankle. She looked at Mouse's ankle. Against the back of Irène's head Mouse's belly touched, moved away, touched, moved away as she breathed. Irène's hand slipped off, came to her lips and then transported a kiss on fingertips back to Mouse's ankle. Then Irène fished a cigarette and then another out of her skirt pocket, lit them and handed one up to Mouse. They smoked and thought for a while.

Mouse said, "Rich people come to the crêperie and I serve them no matter how rich they are. Most are unbeautiful and leave small tips, some leave larger. Yet I do find some of them sympathetic and it would seem silly to try to hate them, wouldn't it? Anyway I probably couldn't."

"I love you, girl."

"I know."

"You don't understand anything, though—you might as well be the national president. Hating them isn't what's needed at all. It's beside the point, really, and I hope you wouldn't be able to hate a person just for being wealthy or love anybody who happens to be poor, the poorer the more. How odd that would be. What we want is not to teach ourselves to hate those to whom the category 'rich' happens to apply, but rather something quite different: to arrange for that category to cease to apply. A world in which there'd be no rich people because there'd be no poor people."

"That's right, I was too stupid."

Only forest animals nearby heard the two women's voices. The nearest other living humans were farther away than a mile—a farm wife, an old farmer grubbing in the earth, a younger farmer riding his tractor this April. Irène's pale eyes slid back and forth from rim to rim of the wide lenses. She sat up. Mouse leaned forward brushing her hands clean.

"Irène?"

"Yes?"

"How do we arrange for that category to cease to apply?"

"We think, we remember, we keep upping the ante. We

keep discovering new ways. We learn to see through, then to discount, then to disregard the welter of lies. We accelerate. We find it less and less necessary to explain and justify what everyone knows whether or not they admit it. We keep waking up. We join hands."

"We're very afraid and sick sometimes though. Aren't we."

"I suppose. Less and less though. Whereas the hopeless are always more so, obviously. If we're afraid we can say we're afraid. Other times we can say we're not afraid. But Mouse there are people made of unending fear who can't even say it, reduced to frozen bright smiles if female, hearty emptiness and empty gravity if male. Open any newspaper. Thank your lucky stars. Some things are clear even if some aren't. Some things are very clear indeed."

"Right. Are you going to dress up tomorrow night?"

"You want me to?"

"I just wondered. Will Jean-Luc and Chantal come to the party?"

"Yes. Jean-Luc anyway and I can't imagine Chantal wouldn't."

"I can."

"Of course. But it would be a declaration of war. Or secession at least. I don't quite see it yet. Does it matter?"

"She lives here."

"In a manner of speaking."

"Goddammit though, Irène, if that's the way, if she doesn't care about anything in the house besides Jean-Luc and her books, if half the time she doesn't manage so much as a good morning to me and when she does it makes me feel like a senile gramps soon to be removed, why be here at all, me? I should go back to my apartment building in Washington. Several times friendly conversations transpired in the entry there. No?"

"Yes a thousand times, you're right, if only it were Christmas, if only this were a sweet U.S. thirties movie instead of life, if only Chantal were a more promising specimen of humanity. If only things were much better than they are, of course, agreed.

"No problem, though, when you stop to think. If at some point you really think you'd be better off back in Washington, wherever, then you'll go. And who knows, I might come with you. Certainly I'd come for a while and from time to time."

"When convenient."

"When possible, Mouse! Heaven help us if you don't know by now that I love you, and that I'll want to be with you as much as I can day-to-day always. I almost worship you, I learn everything from you now. What can . . . ?"

"Okay." Mouse nodded like a child reminding itself of something it must say it believes without believing. Like a child learning a bad lesson. Absently she was touching her nipples. It was a long bitter moment, and then it passed. Mouse began to braid her hair. "I do know you love me. I'm sorry, Irène."

Irène stood and walked across in front of Mouse to a higher boulder. She climbed it and perched there. Mouse stood and stretched.

Irène said, "Without question it is possible for you and me and Jean-Luc (and Chantal if she sticks with us) to find a way to live that doesn't entail leaving somebody out. Or everybody. There must be a good mode. There must be billions, it's only that there's no simple selection procedure and damn little precedent, I think. So what? There are infinite good ways, we try to find one of them. We do not lose hope. Do we Mouse."

"We try our best not to."

"Hungry? I wonder if Gaétan's arrived."

"I think so. Chantal was going to meet his plane because Jean-Luc has to deliver a lecture or something. Gosh, all these violets, I can't believe them."

They were returning by a different route. Mouse led, her head held high. Since Irène watched the ground, picking her footing with care, she sometimes bumped into Mouse who when she had something to say would stop abruptly and speak without turning.

"Did Indians live here, do you know?" Mouse asked.

Irène nodded.

Mouse said, "Someone told me that Indians came to these continents from Russia or China via Alaska. All the way to Tierra del Fuego. Do you think it's true?"

"From what I've read, yes."

"Imagine, Irène."

"Yes."

"I'm not sure, though."

"No. We should get back, Mouse."

"All right. Do you have any stories this weekend?"

"No . . ."

"But a couple."

"No . . ."

"None?"

"Footloose and fancy free."

"For my birthday. I was almost afraid to wonder."

"No you weren't. Oh dear, my darling Oneida girl, your Irène is clumsy in the forest and impatient with town. My legs are short, Mouse. Mouse?"

"This direction."

"Is it hide-and-seek? Speak again."

"I refuse."

"Then how . . . Oh. But it's true we ought to get back."

"I know. Come here on your stubby legs five minutes anyway."

"No. . . ."

"Yes! Otherwise I don't move and you know, dear Irène, you wouldn't find your way home alone. You know you always manage to get lost. Even in Washington you do it."

Irène sighed.

It was six o'clock. Chantal was still in her room. Gaétan and Claude had bathed and rested, come down and, finding no one yet, they had located the liquor cabinet and served themselves cocktails. They were in the living room. Gaétan in an easy chair was leafing through a magazine. Claude stood at the window and looked out. Far down to the left, near the trestle bridge a pair of tiny figures ran out of the woods onto the road.

It had rained, and down there dark and bright puddles gleamed in the clay. The tiny creatures hopped them as they ran weaving and circling up the roadbed apparently in some sort of game for a few minutes until they slowed to a more adult walk. As they came they gesticulated, pointed at a lone oak, the sky, something on the horizon. They stopped to talk, continued, stopped and bent over something in the margin, left it and continued their approach to the house. "Here they are," said Claude. Gaétan came to the window, the magazine under his arm, and set his vermouth on the sill. "The blonde one's Irène," he said.

Introductions performed, more drinks served and music on, the four were in the kitchen. Mouse, Claude and Gaétan sat at the breakfast table and so did Irène when she wasn't carrying out preparations for dinner. The sounds of exclamations and easy laughter moved Chantal to put aside the essay she was writing upstairs and come down and join them. Jean-Luc was later than usual—a meeting had held him up—but eventually he too arrived. Headlights swept across the front of the house and then he came in the back door grinning and glowing, almost dancing into the warm kitchen. There had to be more drinks for his sake. Irène set out bread and butter in case anyone was troubled by the further postponement of dinner.

Mouse lit candles in the dining room and changed the music. She set a nosegay of violets at each place on the table. They might be wilted by midnight but they were pretty on the damask, with the old silver, the old crystal and china. She closed the windows against night breezes. The sky was deep and clear. Her thick hair hung loosely braided down over her shoulders. She wondered who would sit where at dinner. Seating arrangements interested her and often provided secret amusement.

Jean-Luc was leaning against the refrigerator. "So, then, Claude," he said, "which part of France are you from?"

"Not any. I was born in Haarlem. Though I am a quarter Norman and French was spoken in my home."

Gaétan scratched his head. "Jean-Luc, let me think: have you and Irène ever been to Holland? I thought not. You should, so should Mouse and Chantal. You should all come and live there. One of the things that intrigues me most about the Dutch is that almost as a matter of course everyone in cities there speaks one, two or three foreign languages and very fluently. But everyone. Wouldn't you say, Claude? I was astounded. It's understandable, of course, they've always depended on commerce with other peoples. No French or English or U.S. national will learn Dutch so the Dutch learn other people's languages. It's explicable and yet for me it bears a flavor of gallantry."

"How's the food?" Chantal asked.

Irène shrugged. "In a holding pattern."

"No, I meant in Holland."

Claude said, "It's a village cuisine. Resourceful, ample, no nonsense. Lavish with butter, you know. Fish. The good meat all goes to France. Herring. Of course there's an overlay of exotic spices from places like Indonesia."

*

When they moved into the dining room Jean-Luc insisted that Gaétan sit at the head of the table. Irène took the opposite end to be near the doorway to the kitchen and told others to "sit anywhere." Mouse sat at Irène's right. Next to her was Chantal. Facing her, to Gaétan's right, sat Jean-Luc, then Claude facing Mouse, and so back to Irène at her end of the table. Mouse more than the others appreciated the rich manifold of determinants that selected this arrangement from the 720 possible ones.

In view of the dinner she planned for Mouse's birthday tomorrow Irène had kept tonight's comparatively simple— a saucisson d'Arles and then moules marinière, then a gigot with flageolets, a salad and then cheeses. The wines were a rosé from Provence and a côtes-du-Rhone. Irène took a measure of pride in the fact that though it was hardly a risky menu everything was fine. Jean-Luc was happy. He loved Gaétan, their reunions were always a delight and too many years had slipped by since the last. He liked the looks and manner of Gaétan's friend Claude. Chantal was enjoying herself, Irène was in form, and little Mouse seemed content, her dark eyes shining. Jean-Luc held aloft his wineglass. All followed suit. This moment of raised wineglasses and expectant faces turned toward him filled Jean-Luc with joy. "To friendship," he said. "To friendship," in five voices, and crystal touching in the air all around the table.

"Saucisson d'Arles?" said Gaétan. "Wherever did you get it, Irène. And I adore the violets."

"A D.C. charcuterie. You must thank Mouse for the violets."

"Thank you," said Claude.

"Yes," said Mouse. "By the way, do you happen to speak English? I wondered."

"No, I don't. Much of its vocabulary is like Dutch, grammar too, and it's the commonest second language in Holland, but I somehow never acquired it. Gaétan's been interpreting here. You? I suppose you must."

"Sure. But I make too many mistakes by a long shot."

"So do I," said Gaétan. "It doesn't inhibit me though. In fact my impression is that they don't seem to be offended or even quite to notice. This is my first time here and I'm struck by a sort of limbo around their tongue. I'm so inept in it I often quite fail to make myself understood and yet it doesn't seem to matter. They don't ask for clarification. Their faces lapse into a polite vacancy that lasts until the understanding resumes."

Jean-Luc laughed. "You make them sound Chinese, Gaé."

Chantal said, "I know what he means, though. And I assure you, Gaétan, your difficulties with their language have less to do with it than you think. Look, I've known English almost as long as French, and for ordinary purposes ours is barely distinguishable from theirs. And when I talk to them the same kind of thing happens. Much more regularly than in Canada, now that you mention it."

"What does it betoken?" asked Mouse.

There was a brief silence. Gaétan was about to reply when Chantal said, "A touch of mental and spiritual atrophy, I think."

After a moment Irène said, "Genetically defunct Appalachians then, rather than respectful coolies. Where will we touch down next?"

"Arles," said Claude. "It really is a treat, Irène. Jean-Luc, some more for you?"

Good Gaétan, necktie loosened, brow wet already and mopped with his napkin, blooming and beaming at everyone, nodding yes, wagging a forefinger no, bushy eyebrows raised, thinking and dimpling, Gaétan laying a hand over Jean-Luc's or Chantal's forearm as he leaned forward to catch a word of Irène's, and all the while visibly relishing the food and drink, dinner tables were his element. He caught everyone's words with pleasure, all their words. *In fact*... in fact he was responding as Claude had seen him respond to the urban visible in California: as though the dinner were a verbal and prandial L.A. And further, Gaétan's normally remarkable eye seemed to be taking in no more of tonight than his ears and tongue had of the West Coast. Should one question him tomorrow about tonight's visuals one might well draw a blank. The excitement of rejoining comrades after long separation partly accounted for it, of course. Still it was funny.

The interesting candlelight was most active at the table, along rims and turns of silver and crystal, on the fine cloth, and flattering each person transparently and irresistibly. Stiller beyond, out from the table in the whole space of the room it was precise for its dimness. The space was a lozenge with smoothed angles, verticals smoothed by a chimney, a corner cupboard, doors opened into the room, high horizontals smoothed by molding and cobwebs, the lower ones by baseboard and sundry objects. The enclosure opened at two doorways onto the larger living room and kitchen, both dimly lighted with electric incandescent and fluorescent light, onto the fireplace's dark recess, and through the windowpanes onto the April night. Nothing much seemed to dominate—there was an acquiescence. Overall the visual quality was rather finely and effortlessly and very quietly articulated, and at once public and intimate, as at a neighborhood grocer's.

"Gaétan, if you ever wrote us you'd be absolved. We're not letting you off the hook now though. Your father's barber probably knows more about what you've been into than I do."

"But I write, I write. Chantal, don't credit this slander. Mouse, don't listen. You answer my letters, Irène—does your spouse even see them?"

"Usually they're postcards," Irène said. "Appreciated when they come, but Jean-Luc is right in principle: they're more entertaining than informative. Not to put too fine a point on it."

"Ah . . ." sighed Gaétan. "Quiz me then."

"This work of yours, pal," said Jean-Luc.

"As I told Chantal this afternoon, we're a combination research collective and clearing-house, concerned with the visual environment. We've been together for, what is it, Claude—about six years now. Seven of us, all founding members, are a core group. We seven plus two others who've left all lived in the same building at the start, but that's changed. In addition to us seven the group's made up at the moment—and the moment's typical—of twenty-five or so others, half of them in Amsterdam, with widely varying degrees of commitment and so forth. We . . ."

Irène interrupted. "How many are men?"

"Four of the seven, and a little more than half of the others."

"The range of ages?"

Gaétan wagged his finger. "Guess. Or come see. I'm no actuary."

"Do you have group sex?" Jean-Luc wanted to know.

"Claude, we have group sex, don't we? We must, I can't imagine how we could have managed this long without it."

"Or show your faces. But what else is it you do?"

"As I said. We gather and distribute information about visual environments. Film and videotape are the media of choice but we also use still photos and slides. We publish a resource catalogue, sponsor and do research, and of course there's a fair amount of paperwork—annotation and commentary on projects, correspondence with interested parties, especially the similarly oriented groups we know of—Stockholm, Tokyo and one in Los Angeles.

"We're concerned almost exclusively with the urban environment. For a number of reasons, but suffice it to say that the need for documentation there is most urgent just now because irreversible visual change is currently proceeding at a much faster rate in cities than elsewhere."

Chantal's and Mouse's glances chanced to meet. As a rule when it happened both pairs of eyes lost focus and moved, but tonight it made Chantal break into a smile and nearly made Mouse do the same.

"I like this rosé," Mouse said. "Do you?"

"Yes I do. Let's see where...." Chantal rotated the bottle. "Cavalaire."

Irène went to the kitchen and returned carrying a tray so heaped with steaming mussels that her arms trembled and she walked quickly.

"You must be the P.R. man," she said. "What about funding? I'm intrigued."

"Hmm. Well, we rent and sell our productions to universities or anyone who wants them. Libraries subscribe to the catalogue and some bookstores and periodical outlets retail it." Claude touched the edge of her plate with the foot of her wineglass. "And a couple of the members who're loaded made donations at the founding. It's really pretty cushy."

Irène nodded. "And, uh... how does disbursement work?"

"Fixed salary for full-time—all equal—plus expenses. Expenses and hour- or piece-wages for part-time. There's a rainy day stash, otherwise all funds are disbursed with semiannual budgeting."

"Congratulations," said Irène. "Not bad. Rather better than I expected, I must admit."

"She means no offense, Claude," said Gaétan. "Her intentions are good—forgive her manner, chalk it up to her practice of journalism. Though if truth be told..."

"Fiddlesticks," said Irène. "I want to know your criteria for success. Your reasons, what you profess, why you do what you do. Mere documentation seems . . . frivolous."

Gaétan smiled. "Hence in character? I adore you, Irène, I always have. If only this rascal" (gesturing toward Jean-Luc) "hadn't taken unfair advantage, knowingly too, of your misattribution of my . . ."

"The balloons!" Jean-Luc shook his head. "Good heavens, Gaé, I haven't thought about those balloons in years. Have you, Irène?"

The silly story of the balloons was recounted by the principals with interruptions, conflicting testimony, protestations and denials, the other three cross-examining and conferring among themselves in lowered voices, and then the talk turned again to Gaétan's work. Irène pressed for a rationale, Claude deferred to Gaétan, but he had explained all he would that evening. He suggested that Irène rent a videotape the group had made of itself discussing itself.

Mouse said, "Gaétan, may I ask you something?"

"You, Mouse? Anything, the sky's the limit."

"More than I need, but thanks. I was wondering why you didn't come here sooner."

"I've been asking myself the same thing. I'd have been here years ago on the double if Irène had done you any justice—if she'd ventured beyond the merest mention of you. Chantal would've brought me too, but I wasn't even aware of her existence. Jean-Luc and Irène waste their best drawing cards. I'd have been here with bells on."

"Ah," said Jean-Luc, "the smoothness of his tongue. But it's forked, Mouse, Chantal, don't be taken for a ride. Nothing under the sun would have dragged him here before it pleased him to be magnetized by California—nothing, not even you."

"By-blows, is it?" said Chantal.

Mouse was wearing hiking boots, faded dungarees and a white cotton tee shirt. Unobtrusively she moved her left hand around out of Irène's or anyone else's line of sight to touch a folded slip of thin paper in her hip pocket.

"What do you hear from Serge?" Jean-Luc asked.

"He was one of our band in Paris in the old days," Irène explained. "For a year or so he and Jean-Luc and Gaé and I and two or three others were together most of our free time. Serge went off to Toulouse to live with a woman, found some sort of work—representing a publishing house, as I remember. He rented a beautiful old cottage out from the city on the river. The rest of us went down once or twice to visit him and . . . Marie-France, wasn't it? Anyway then Jean-Luc and I came to the U.S. and we lost touch."

"He was a closer friend of mine than of yours, I think," Gaétan said. "We grew closer after you'd left. Marie-France was good for him. He was something of a recluse by nature, you know, and she understood and accepted that. They seemed to have found their nook, didn't they? And I counted on being able to come back always. I thought that when I was sixty, no matter what was happening I'd still be going to Toulouse now and again to visit. I suppose I assumed they'd have bought the cottage by then. I don't think they had any children in the future I'd counted on.

"But then, not long after you and Irène left France,

someone heard that they had given up the cottage and gone to Italy and that they were planning to return to Paris to live. Half a year went by, a year, no word. I wrote to Toulouse but they'd left no forwarding address. Another year passed. Sometimes when there was an unexpected knock at my door, when the phone rang at an odd hour I'd be sure it was Serge. It never was. Marie-France's family had been in Grasse but I don't think I'd ever known her last name, nor did anybody else. And for all I know she and Serge might no longer have been together anyway. Serge himself had no family.

"When I'm back in Paris I inquire whenever I run into anyone who knew him. Nobody's heard a thing. Frustrating, isn't it? . . . disheartening. Well, I tell myself it's symptomatic of our world and time, how we live. Fraught with losing track somehow. I still do half harbor a hope that one day yet I'll see Serge ambling down our Rue Mouffetard again."

Jean-Luc looked into the candle flames, rubbing a thumb across his moustache. "A sad story, Gaétan. Makes me think of wartime. I don't like it so very much."

Mouse shrugged.

Irène was rising to clear for the next course when Jean-Luc stood and said, "Let me, Irène." People lit cigarettes, the remainder of the rosé was downed. Sweet raindrops splattered against the windowpanes, a momentary shower, more wind than rain stirring branches, new leaves, barely wetting the grass. Jean-Luc cleared the table, brought the main course and the côtes-du-Rhone, and proceeded to carve the gigot. Mouse went to the living room to change the music.

The wind had gone out of earshot, Jean-Luc had served everyone and filled wineglasses. Softly with wonderful verisimilitude a Chopin waltz ended in the room beyond. Into the ensuing silence from outside, not far, came an uncannily human cry, frightful and lovely and long, the next waltz had begun and was taking shape when it ceased.

"Jeepers!" said Gaétan. "What in heaven's name?"

Jean-Luc nodded, smiling.

"Don't be alarmed," said Chantal. "It's a kind of owl."

"We don't hear him but two or three nights a year. I don't know why. Chances are though he'll call again tonight."

"He's welcoming you," said Mouse. "Irène, we heard him when we were snowbound, remember?"

"Welcoming?" said Gaétan.

Claude said, "Of course one would get snowbound here. Was it fun?"

Jean-Luc raised his eyebrows. "It could all too easily have been dangerous. We were isolated for five or six days and..."

Irène interrupted. "But don't romanticize, Jean-Luc. If we really had needed anything we'd have telephoned for it."

"But what if the telephone lines had been down? Anyway what good would telephoning for help have done? The roads would still have been blocked. We could have died before an overland expedition got through." Jean-Luc nodded with an air of having scored the telling point against Irène. Irène smiled. Jean-Luc went on, "Anyway yes,

Claude, it was enjoyable. Lots of Simenon, you know. I diddled a bit with Molière but it was too good a time to waste on workaday business."

"I should think. What besides Simenon?—I'm curious. Poetry maybe," said Gaétan.

"Ten years ago it would have been, wouldn't it? But you know, Gaé, I fear I'm finding that for me at least age has made my appetite for it dwindle. Gee, what was it I was reading?"

"Garcia Marquez, and you liked it," said Irène. "I did too."

Mouse said, "*Black Elk Speaks.*"

"Ah, it comes back. Yes, and I liked that too. Debray's conversations with Allende. And *La naissance du jour.* What a fine thing that is. I'd not read it before, either."

Gaétan said, "It really is like heaven's grace, isn't it, coming across something fine for the first time at our age. Almost enough to make you advocate systematic withholding of a few treasures. So, Jean-Luc, it sounds a fair read for six days."

It had been. For more than a decade Jean-Luc had read detective novels steadily, one or two a week, but otherwise his reading was in spurts like the snowbound one, separated by intervals as long as six or eight months with nothing but his professional reading—scholarly books and journal articles—newspapers and magazines and the detective fiction. Earlier he had read more. Indeed in adolescence and childhood he'd been a bit of a bookworm. Then more than now he had read slowly and thoughtfully and often stopped in the middle of a sentence to brood on it.

From an early age he had read with a sophistication never achieved in the lives of the great majority of readers in his world. At an early age he passed beyond culling alter egos and roles from books, beyond those dodges. He had come to read with such sophistication that the vicissitudes of fictional people could hold his most serious attention and he could be healed or hurt by a mere story's unfolding. When it came to reading to acquire information, bodies of facts, he was less adept. He did little nonprofessional reading of poetry. It was partly because with poems more than with other sorts of texts he willy-nilly grew professional, saw the work in terms of journal articles, university posts, academic careers. In the old days in Paris, though, he and Irène and Gaétan had lived with poems as with lovers, sought out poetry at bouquinistes, in cafes, as did many young and old Parisians.

"Of course you'd have been without newspapers," Chantal said.

"Yes. Irène was at loose ends but I think the rest of us enjoyed it."

Gaétan said, "Irène, when I see your byline a thousand questions pop into my head. Like: Are you well-paid? How much editing gets done after the piece leaves your hands? Do all the pieces you send in get published? What percent does? How much of what you cover is assigned, how much your choice? To what extent and in what ways do editorial positions and other such forces shape and color what comes off your typewriter? I guess the general question is, how free does the press look from inside?"

"How free does it look from outside?"

"Hmm."

"It looks like that from inside too."

"But there must be degrees."

"Yes, yes of course. Our press is less controlled than the Russian and even the U.S. ones, and some of our papers are less controlled than others. At any paper some staffs are less controlled than others. Any staff is more at liberty with some stories than others. There are degrees upon degrees, a wealth of fine shadings. And I suppose they're worth being aware of."

"Yes they are. Heaven help us, of course—inside or outside the profession."

"But I assure you that if freedom is Z all these are shadings from F to H. The very lexicon from which the crossword puzzle on the back page is constructed is under an array of constraints. Do I need to point it out? Or that as things stand infractions are impossible since the owners have too many well-separated and more or less pocketed groups between the puzzle-maker and the readership? Or that the constraints are never, god knows, admitted to the public and practically never even within the profession? In fact, although we all, whatever we do, have them down cold, I suspect few of us ever let ourselves be conscious of them, not even when we're drifting off to sleep. Do November bears understand what they've been at since March—the bicycles and tutus?"

"No," said Mouse. "But Irène, would you describe Z?"

"It would be free," said Irène.

"Would the crossword puzzles be easier?" Jean-Luc asked. "Would they be better?"

Gaétan said, "Would there be crossword puzzles?"

Irène said, "Claude, what do you suppose—would there?"

But before Claude could speak Jean-Luc said, "Irène didn't let you off the hook, Gaétan. Do we let her off?"

Irène leaned back tilting up her face, smiling, her eyes coasting all around the table. "Okay, all right. Yes, there'll be crossword puzzles. Easier in some respects and harder in others. And better."

Claude said, "Precisely what I would have said. She took the words out of my mouth. By the way, Irène, my impression's been that the Dutch press at the moment is well to the H of G. Would you agree?"

Irène nodded. "In fact it's—aieee...." It was the owl's cry again. Was it a mating call? If so, why such long waits between for a response? And for a mating call it sounded too... disinterested, sequestered. Yet what other function might it serve? It came from the same direction and nearness as before. The six people at dinner found themselves almost smiling to hear it and think of its feathers, soft and dun in color and soft in flight. The rich lamb, the flageolets' back-of-the-tongue dullness like earth, the room cool enough so that one came peculiarly alive to the darkness of the hearth, one couldn't quite be altogether comfortable and yet one knew that a fire there now wouldn't be pleasant either, in April it was too late for other than candle flames—these things might almost have been the subject of the owl's cry.

*

Gaétan said, "But isn't it odd, Irène, knowing that anything you write that's published is to have a lifespan of exactly twenty-four hours?"

"The extent of the readership offsets the fast obsolescence though, doesn't it?" Chantal said. "Poor Jean-Luc. . . ."

He nodded. "With luck the monograph I've published won't be obsolete for a generation or so, but who reads it? In a single day Irène's work commands more reader-hours than that monograph in its whole life."

"You mean you should become a journalist too?" Mouse asked.

Irène said, "Out of the question." She went to the kitchen and returned with the salad, passing through the living room on the way to change the music. Leaning toward Chantal, Gaétan was saying, "So tell me about Montréal—would I like it?"

Chantal crossed her legs and shifted from one hipbone to the other. She was eating pieces of salad with her fingers—she shook drops of oil and vinegar off the frilly lettuce onto her plate. Around her neck was a velvet choker with a cameo. She said, "I'll always have a soft spot in my head for Montréal, I suppose. When I was growing up I couldn't wait for the Girl Scout trips away—it was the only time I left. I thought any city must basically be Montréal—I accepted the fact that in some of them the populace had yellow skin and spoke Chinese but that was only a kind of play they indulged in. So I didn't especially regret not having seen other cities. What I looked forward to were the scout trips into the bush, camping out. Anyway yes, I think you'd find it pleasant. Overly so maybe, I don't know. Nowadays in parts of the old town, Place Cartier, there's lots of street life, healthier than down here I think. Open cafés with everybody singing bawdy songs, you know, good-natured cruising and flânerie."

"She makes it sound very attractive," said Claude.

"Doesn't she. I've never been there myself."

Gaétan waved his salad fork. "Speaking of places, only this afternoon I was reading in a magazine of yours about an explosive specialist, an interesting type who'd been envisioning ways to leave the earth."

"I recall it," Irène said. "But it was several months ago, wasn't it?"

"Yes. I was reading it when you and Mouse came back from the woods so I didn't finish. Anyway his idea was that chemical reactions are unconscionably feeble and inefficient energy sources for travelling away from this planet. He proposed instead to use nuclear explosions in series. According to him, with this method it will be feasible, even simple, to move Chicago to the moon. He also suggests dismantling Jupiter and using it to make a sphere enclosing the sun and the inner planets to collect all the sun's radiant energy. As things stand we have the use of only the minute fraction absorbed by this planet."

"Sounds like a good idea," said Chantal. "Why didn't anyone think of it before?"

Mouse tried to conceal how surprised she was by this kind of talk as she said, "People walk on the moon already."

"Not enough, not easily enough, according to the guy in the article. The moon's small potatoes. He expects to fly through the sun's corona, visit the outer planets in his lifetime. And what really interests him is longer trips to other stars."

"To what end?" Jean-Luc asked.

"The fun of it?"

Mouse lit a cigarette. "Maybe," she said, "he expects to meet other kinds of people."

"He wouldn't be alone," said Irène. "Creeping extraterrestrialism's plaguing the media. The vogue's been analyzed to death too—some say it comes in waves, some say it's a response to the sordid decline our own world seems to be suffering."

Gaétan said, "Frankly, I've always assumed that I and all my friends, all my dinner companions, must be Martians."

Mouse glanced toward the windows. She was unable to treat the subject lightly. "What should we do?" Her question wasn't understood. "What must we do about the people from other worlds?" The question was understood now but for several seconds it went unanswered—perhaps it was laughable. Then Irène said, "Wish them well. And hope that it won't take more than twenty thousand years to greet and help each other. What's to say? Are you afraid they'd scorn you, Mouse? They wouldn't if they were wise."

After a moment Gaétan said, "What intrigued me more in the article was what the fellow had to say about the likelihood of nuclear bombs being built by insurgents. He tells how to make one and it doesn't sound difficult. He gives examples of what could be done with a homemade fission bomb and it's awesome, almost enough to make you want not to live in cities."

Jean-Luc clapped his friend on the shoulder. "All this in English, Gaétan!"

Gaétan smiled. "At last. I was afraid I'd have to mention it myself."

"He's shameless," said Chantal, and Irène and Mouse agreed. Chantal had cleared the table and brought the cheese. She was serving strong coffee and cognac.

Presently Claude went up to bed. Soon after, Chantal did the same, then Gaétan and then Jean-Luc. Chantal was half-asleep when Jean-Luc crawled into bed beside her. "Hi." It was warm and snug and sexy—Jean-Luc had an erection but he was too tired to make love. So was Chantal. "Nice dinner," she said. "Is the weekend over?"

"Yes," said Jean-Luc, "except for another dinner tomorrow and then Mouse's party on Sunday."

Irène and Mouse stayed below to tidy up. "These dishes!" Irène said. "We should have made Jean-Luc and Chantal do them, for the principal of the thing. Well, I'll leave tomorrow's for them, and Sunday is Jean-Luc's show so it's fair enough."

"What's Sunday?"

"I must've told you—some people from Jean-Luc's department coming for dinner. By then we'll be zombies anyway so perhaps we won't notice."

"Would you like some music now, Irène?"

"I'm not sure. If you want something, put it on, but not too loud."

"No . . . it's nice without sometimes too. What's a Pap smear?"

Irène explained. She had made appointments for herself and Mouse and Chantal to have the test and had announced as much on a scrap of paper affixed to the bulletin board Mouse was perusing. Mouse had never had a Pap smear. Irène had them erratically. As she described the simple test and its purpose she tried for the right balance of earnestness and off-handedness.

Irène washed the dishes in two shifts with a break between for the first rackful to dry enough to be put away. Mouse swept the floor and then, though there was other work she might have done, she sat in a straight-backed chair tilted against the wall, with a glass of wine. She pretended not to watch Irène so as not to make her self-conscious, Irène at the sink with the sleeves of her green silk shirt rolled above her elbows. Doubtless Irène supposed she was working very efficiently and was taking a minor private pleasure in the thought but in truth she was washing dishes the way a child does, taking absurd pains without yet leaving any object quite clean. Mouse loved it, she loved to see Irène good-humored and tired and inept this way. She loved Irène and pretended not to watch her. Locusts were singing outside, now and then a doubtful breeze rose and fell, upstairs no one was making love apparently, it sounded as if they were all sleeping.

Irène wanted to know what Mouse thought of Gaétan. Mouse liked him, his laughter and bright eyes, his flyaway dandruffy hair. Had she expressed reservations, Irène would surely have leapt to his defense with an attack on Mouse's judgement. As it was she felt called to remind Mouse that Gaétan's charm was frivolous. "He wouldn't last a day in the bush"—but even Irène had to smile at that. Claude had impressed them favorably. They both liked the compliant judiciousness with which she had eaten and talked through the meal. Would Claude survive long in the bush? Longer than Gaétan, they concluded. "Tell me about your grandmother," Irène said when she had finished the dishes, lit a cigarette and sat in a chair near Mouse's looking at the floor. Mouse told of her grandmother's canine and crystalline voice in the doorway, "Ot-si-no-wa! Help me work my deerskin," or late at night through a window, "Ot-si-no-wa, the corn dance!" Nothing had made the woman happier than sewing patches—Mouse remembered dish towels that were all patchwork without a trace of the original cloth. Irène listened. Mouse described her grandmother's bread and dreams the old woman had recounted. Irène breathed easier, deeper and slower, listening. After a while they too went up to bed, extinguishing lights as they moved through the house.

It was ten-thirty when Jean-Luc began to waken. The room was full of pale sunlight. Chantal slept like a child under the yellow blanket. Jean-Luc sat up, swung one and then the other leg out over the edge. He stood and yawned, stretching, a fine figure of a naked man in the diffuse morning light. His dungarees were on the desk chair, he picked them up in one hand. Open on the desk were notes for a lecture he was to deliver next week. He picked them up and began reading them over. The dungarees fell unnoticed into a heap against his ankle on the floor. With the hand that had held them Jean-Luc scratched his head, rumpling the lustrous black hair. The hand rested there a moment, came around across his chest and scratched under the arm holding the paper. Then it slid down across his navel, slowed and gave one, then another, then a third light thwack with the palm to his lower abdomen as he read. It came down, cupped loosely and gave a light waking-up jiggle to his genitals, rested there a moment and then came up, took the paper from his other hand and replaced it on the desk. Sleepy Jean-Luc stood there foolishly until he felt something against his ankle. It was his dungarees. What were they doing on the floor? Chantal slept like a baby, curled under the lemon-yellow blanket.

Downstairs with a mug of strong coffee, waiting for an English muffin, he was more awake. Near the toaster was something annoying, a tiny clay vase with a greasy wishbone, some dried weeds and a feather in it. Annoying because it must be Mouse's or something she had given Irène, it must have some sentimental significance and therefore couldn't be tossed out for the junk it was. In fact, hadn't it been there for weeks, months maybe? Jean-Luc sighed. He had buttered and was biting into a muffin when Chantal tiptoed into the room. She wore the muslin smock she used as a peignoir. Jean-Luc watched her tiptoe across the floor and then he swallowed and said, "Good morning." She sat on his lap and put her thin arms around his neck, her face against his.

Irène entered the room and stopped, as surprised as they. For an instant nobody spoke or moved, then Chantal slid her arms from Jean-Luc's neck and said, "Hi. Anyone else up?"

Irène said, "I think Gaétan and Claude are asleep, Mouse is still in bed but she's awake, I thought I was the first down." In a black turtleneck, blue denim wraparound, she barefoot too, she went to the stove as she spoke and clicked on the burner under a kettle.

Chantal said, "Could you see if there's enough for me?"

Irène shook the kettle. "Bold as brass, is it?" she thought. "Brazen it out this morning perched on his lap like a movie floozie? Your little pig's heart must be stumbling over itself. Unfortunately you didn't quite bring it off, though. Why don't you run through it again with more sugar on the voice—more gloat and taunt, you know. Some animation in the face wouldn't be amiss either, and you might try unzipping his fly as you mouth the line. Imagine the way an adult might do it." Then she thought, "Steady, Irène, it's not worth it."

Chantal brought two cups with spoonfuls of freeze-dried coffee in them to the stove. "You must've done the kitchen last night. I was going to do it this morning."

"Did you enjoy the dinner?" Irène asked. The kettle was whistling, a long plume stood out from it. Irène poured lively water and set the kettle on a cold burner—when water remaining in the aluminum hemisphere sloshed, the lid's aperture emitted a gentle "Whew."

Jean-Luc had returned his attention to the newspaper. Chantal picked up another section of it and sat across the table from him. Irène opened the refrigerator door, hiding them, and lifted out a four-kilo salmon wrapped in fishmarket paper which she laid on a counter. She squatted before a lower bank of cabinets and began to extricate a roasting pan from the jumble of other metal receptacles lodged there. It couldn't have been done much less noisily but the crash and clatter at that hour was disconcerting to those who hadn't expected it. Jean-Luc frowned and for the moment Chantal didn't exist, there was only Irène's noise when one was trying to read something inconsequential in peace, routing one's dregs of sleepiness at a stroke, and why? How did one find oneself in such a plight? It was too characteristic. "What are you doing, Irène?" God damn it all. Chantal resented his tone, his wife's polished face. Extravagances like overturning the table flooded her mind but she resolved instead to sip her coffee and keep reading the paper like a mother whose children have fought too often for her to notice any more. Jean-Luc was frowning. Irène didn't move but her eyes seemed to wheel toward him. "Peeing," she said. "I thought there might be some toilet tissue in here but I don't see any." She said it thinking that an ace reporter, a free agent, a knowledgeable and intelligent woman could afford some buffoonery if anyone could. Then she said, "No," stood and stood with her hand resting on the fish, because in a flash she saw it wasn't right, in front of witnesses it was coming across wrong and never mind whether the fault was hers or theirs, people get locked up for such things. If only Chantal weren't there, she thought. She patted the wrapped fish. "I have to poach it now for it to have time to chill. The salmon."

"Come off it, don't be ridiculous," Jean-Luc said.

Chantal was puzzled. "But Irène, it can't take more than six or eight hours, can it?"

"Of course not," said Jean-Luc. "I can't believe this."

"It's for Mouse's birthday," Irène said in a very loud voice.

Jean-Luc sighed. "We know that Irène. That's the point."

Chantal scratched her head. "Wait, but . . ."

"My god," said Jean-Luc. "Mouse's birthday *is* tomorrow isn't it? Irène?"

Irène stopped and gave the roasting pan a furious tug, freeing it and also a skillet which went skidding across the floor. "It begins to make sense," she said. "I see now why we're having your colleagues tomorrow. A sort of buffer zone to protect you."

Jean-Luc smiled. "But you're ready to believe worse, aren't you? Oh Irène, goddamnit, those people are coming tonight, not tomorrow!"

"No. . . ."

"Yes."

"A pretty pickle," said Chantal.

Thinking fast, Jean-Luc considered and then rejected proposing that the birthday party be postponed. He said, "I'm sure you told me it was tomorrow but I guess you didn't. I'm sorry, Irène, I really am." Irène had been thinking fast too and was on the point of offering to telephone Jean-Luc's colleagues and tell them their dinner was off, but what Jean-Luc said, the honest way he said it made her reconsider. "What about food?"

Chantal said, "Can the menus be combined—less of more for all? Let's see...." The idea was a good one, it would work.

While Irène poached her fish and returned it to the refrigerator Chantal and Jean-Luc carried out other preparations for the meal. Mouse assisted when she came down and so a little later did Claude and Gaétan. Around two they went out for a walk. Gaétan proposed it, there was some initial resistance but his absurd bustling insistence prevailed. The grass was wet and one could feel rain in the air, it was cool and sunny with puffs of white everywhere in the blue. Luckily no shower broke. They followed the old stage track and then cut back through the woods along a rocky stream. Mouse was wading, she turned over a rock and beckoned for Gaétan to look. "Good heavens, écrevisses?" She nodded solemnly. Everyone came to see. In their unhurried progress through the woods and then out onto the gravel road precisely where Irène and Mouse had appeared to Claude's view yesterday and so up to the house, one pattern recurred as a norm in the slow flux of groupings, singlings and pairings—Mouse ahead, then Claude and Irène, followed by Gaétan and Jean-Luc, with Chantal bringing up the rear. Jean-Luc and Gaétan walked together laughing and talking as they'd have done through the night in the old days. It was four-thirty when they came out onto the road and began the ascent to the ordinary. They saw a strange car there and a group of people sitting on the porch steps. It was ever so slightly ominous until from nearer Jean-Luc recognized one of them, a boy from one of his classes. That one waved.

His name was Brad. He and Mimmy, Rosie, Craig and Jeff, en route to the capital to catch a rock concert at D. A. R. Hall, were dropping in to say hello and have a look at the place, see how a prof lived. There was a silence. "Let's go inside," Jean-Luc said in English. "*Si*," said Jeff, who was learning Spanish.

Chantal slipped away to do some reading, Claude went up for a nap, Irène excused herself to see to the dinner. Everybody else was in the living room. Craig and Jeff, it turned out, were undergraduates like Brad. The three had met in a fraternity Brad and Jeff had since dropped out of, out of which Craig hadn't dropped though he was considering it. Mimmy and Rosie had dropped out of colleges outside Virginia and returned to Charlottesville where they and Craig grew up and where they now worked as waitresses in two of the better restaurants. "Mouse is waitressing too," Jean-Luc explained. "In Washington." Since September the five had lived in a house that was part of an estate of Mimmy's father's. Brad's French was serviceable but in deference to his companions who spoke little or none—it was Greek to Jeff—conversation was mostly in English.

"Nice place you've got here, sir," said Brad. "You own it or rent it?"

Jean-Luc explained that it was rented and, having performed the requisite introductions, asked who would like what to drink.

"Anything's fine," said Mimmy. "I assume you meant something alcoholic."

Craig said, "We smoked some dope while we were waiting for you to show up. It's pretty good, if anybody wants any."

"It's *very* good—I'm out of my skull," said Rosie.

Gaétan said, "I think you're the first U.S. nationals of your age I've met. Are you a representative sample?" There was a flurry of glances at this.

Jean-Luc smiled. "He has to be humored. Crème de la crème, Gaé. He intends no insult."

"Oh obviously. I only meant in terms of things like interests, height, race, family background—you know, value-free terms. It's a silly question anyhow."

Brad opined that it was actually an interesting question but that a careful answer would take till midnight or beyond. "It would be like us asking you if you're a representative sample—in those kinds of terms—of your age-group of Frenchmen."

Rosie sniggered.

After a moment Mimmy said, "What's funny? You're making me paranoid."

"No," said Rosie, "I was just looking at my feet and trying to figure what they're representative samples of, that's all."

"Fetishists' dream feet come true?" said Mimmy.

Rosie sniggered again and said, "Or vice versa."

Mimmy said, "She's stoned okay," pointing with a thumb.

"How do you people like America?" asked Craig.

Gaétan said, "Mouse? You're the only one of us who's been in South and North America both."

Craig said, "*We've* never been in *South* America. I was referring to the United States of America, if you can understand."

"I've been to Nassau though, everybody has," said Mimmy.

Jeff nodded. "Europe too, as far as that goes. I could dig South America though if I didn't get sick."

"That's right, isn't it," said Rosie. "Maybe it'd be worth it though. It's probably an interesting place."

Craig said, "We're off the subject. These foreigners were going to give us an idea of how they like it here, remember? You sir for instance," Craig said, leaning forward toward Gaétan, "How do you find it in comparison to France?"

Gaétan sucked at the joint handed him, held the smoke in his lungs and then said, "It seems more spread out." Craig nodded. Gaétan continued, "I've only been here three weeks. I'd always thought of the U.S. as . . . durable, you know? Young yes but a fairly permanent entity. I don't know if you understand me but, whether or not it's justified, one finds it simply inconceivable that there should ever not be a France, ever ever. So I'd thought of your nation in roughly the same way. But since I've actually been here in it, Craig, to my surprise and delight it's often impressed me as rather fleeting and evanescent, fragile, you know? And nothing like so necessary and permanent as France—where incidentally I haven't lived for a number of years."

"Where have you lived?"

"Amsterdam."

"What's your view, sir?" Brad asked Jean-Luc. Jean-Luc

liked the boy whom he privately called "the good soldier" because of the valor he showed in class, his readiness to shoulder any and all burdens assigned him, his generosity and the near-mythic shine of his scrubbed cheeks—"the good soldier" affectionately with some sadness as if he were committed to doing wrong with the best will in the world— the stalwart Brad, always looking as if he had just come from the barber's. Jean-Luc wouldn't quite have guessed that this boy lived in a house with young women like Mimmy and stoned Rosie. Was one of them his lover? What would Brad become in two, three decades? What did such superhuman cleanliness promise? Jean-Luc wondered. "My view?"

"He lives here," said Mimmy with a shrug.

"He still might have a view anyway," said Jeff.

"He's probably taciturn," said Rosie without taking her eyes off her knees—as if there were a little television screen there showing something moderately interesting.

Gaétan said, "Out with it, Jean-Luc."

Jean-Luc sighed. "I might say that I find it easy to live here, easier than lots of places I could name, but that I don't find it easy to be at ease here and I doubt that many others do, be they citizen or mere resident, and I decline to speculate about why."

"Dope helps," said Rosie. "Hooch, music."

Mouse, who'd been finding Rosie decidedly funny and attractive, asked her, "Do you enjoy being a waitress?"

"It's okay," said Rosie. "It's better than being a student."

"Being a student sucks," said Craig.

"Being a student's okay," said Brad.

"Shit!" cried Mimmy. "Look what the fuck time it is. We

won't have time for shopping before the concert if we don't get on the stick, really."

Jean-Luc went with them out to their car. "I hope you'll come back. It's good to see you outside class, Brad, it's a pleasure to meet all of you. Do drop in again before you graduate."

"Who knows, maybe we will," said Rosie.

"It's a nice place you've got here," Craig said. "The rent's probably reasonable too, this far out."

Brad said, "Thank you, sir, we will."

Car doors slammed. "Bye," said Mimmy.

Jeff said, "*Adios,*" and tooted the horn as he drove off. "Otsinowa sounds almost more Indian, like American Indian, than French to me."

"She looked sort of Indian too," said Rosie. "So, Brad, will that get you an A or did we blow it?"

"Search me. How about starting another joint? You okay to drive, Jeff?"

"Yes but . . ."

"Left here, man."

Mouse was sitting under the black walnut tree. Jean-Luc smiled at her and smoothed back her long hair. "Happy Birthday."

"Thanks. By the way, which one is your student?"

"Brad, the boy with shoes like moccasins. I can't imagine how they found this place. Did you mind them?"

"I enjoyed them," said Mouse.

"Good. I hope they enjoyed us. I don't know whether you noticed, Mouse, but the one called Craig couldn't take his eyes off you."

"I tried not to notice."

"The girls were nice, Rosie especially. Well then." Jean-Luc strolled with his hands in his pockets back into the house. It was quiet, the living room was empty. As he stacked glasses he took cognizance of the fact that back in the kitchen Irène and Gaétan were talking in lowered voices. Jean-Luc set the glasses on the mantelpiece and went up to tell Chantal about the young visitors.

Gaétan was chopping apples, Irène had pre-heated the oven and prepared a goose for stuffing, she was smoking a cigarette and watering small bromeliads on the windowsill. "It's like jealousy I suppose, but that's not really quite what it is," she said. "Jean-Luc thinks I'm jealous, and so for that matter do Chantal and Mouse, but they're mistaken. Unless I misunderstand the word. I don't mind Jean-Luc's fucking Chantal, I don't even object to his loving her, *per se*. This is true, Gaé. Once half by chance I walked in on them while they were in the middle of making love, there was something or other I had to discuss with Jean-Luc. Anyway I felt no anxiety about it, you know?" Gaétan tossed a handful of apple cubes into his mouth. Irène continued, "So, it isn't really jealousy that's driven me up walls on occasion. It's more resentment at a kind of stupidity or unfairness on Jean-Luc's part."

"Explain."

"Mmm. Exclusiveness, I guess. Sometimes he behaves as if the point of his affair is to shut me out. That's the effect in any case. Magical walls spring up between him and me when she's present. Proscriptions and taboos of the most ordinary things. When we're alone we're pretty much the way we always were, but let her walk into the room and up go the force fields—I'm not free to touch him even, or if I do it amounts to a violation, almost a violence. It sounds insane but it's how we've lived since she came. It's not so bad lately—ugh!, in the beginning it was frightful. Another form the exclusiveness takes is wilful deafness, refusal to hear me say almost anything beyond comments on weather. I tried to get through to him, begged him to let me talk to him. Nothing worked so finally I gave up. Well, and lately things are improving there too. He seeks me out, creates opportunities for us to talk. I play it cool, willing but not especially eager. He in his cautious way touches on this or that delicate subject—reopening them, signalling that some of the censorship is relaxing. God damn him, Gaétan, I love him so much I can hardly believe it, and do you know what I hate about him? He's scared to death of me. I hate it, I hate it. I don't even understand it. I'm the least frightening person in the world.

"Well, as I say, I think we're finding our way out of such looniness. In any case I don't think any of that has to do with jealousy quite."

"No? No, I guess not."

"No, because sex isn't at issue, not even love, at least not Jean-Luc's for Chantal. If I stop to think about it I suppose in an abstract way I'm envious of the affection and interest he shows her but I really seldom think anything about her. Apples done? Okay, let's stuff it. It's a relief to be able to talk to someone besides Mouse about all this. I've unloaded too many of these stupidities on her. She's very good, Gaétan."

"She's charming. Is Jean-Luc . . ."

"Jealous of her? Of course, of course he is. Or was. Though as you might guess he suffered nobly and secretly—so much that for some time I didn't have an inkling." Irène was trussing the goose. Gaétan stood beside her gazing out at the pretty afternoon light, sipping his good vermouth.

He said, "I was thinking about years, how accidental and arbitrary they are, years, centuries, and so forth. All a year is is the amount of time it takes for this particular planet to make a complete circuit of its particular sun, that's all. So it's awfully provincial of us, really, to think of a year as a sort of average or normal length of time and of, say, three million years as a longish time."

Irène smiled. "It's in comparison to three score and ten."

"I know. I was thinking that even assuming we're finite-lived, assuming we must die, our life spans need not be a function of a sum of our planet's round trips. I was thinking that we might slow ourselves somehow—cool ourselves or something so that everything happening in our bodies would happen much more slowly—thoughts, molecular changes, everything. Slow everything on the planet. Then we might live three million years instead of seventy, if we chose. Trees would live six million, dogs only a million. Our finest instruments wouldn't be able to record the old flicker of day and night probably. Years then would be almost nothing, wouldn't they—maybe a sort of shimmer in our field of vision we'd notice when we were outdoors, whatever. A butterfly then would live longer than we do now."

"A butterfly couldn't fly that slowly," Irène said. "An owl certainly couldn't—one wingbeat every ten years?"

"Well, maybe we could thicken the air or something. Otherwise we'd have to lighten all flying things, I suppose. Activities involving missiles—sports, warfare—might not be the same either. But I should think the differences could be minimized. And what I was wondering is, why should we want to live three million instead of seventy years if all it amounted to was a difference in the outdoor lighting? Why not instead speed everything up, give ourselves a lifetime of a second or two? All the future history of the race, assuming *it's* finite, might occur then in an hour or two, maybe much less. That way everybody could move to the sunny side. I don't know. The only reasons I could come up with for bothering to live at a different rate were, first that if the U.S. and Soviet power structures keep meeting as little resistance as they now do, it might be wise to slow things to give us better odds of being rescued by people from other planets before we've all been eliminated by CIA and KGB operatives. The other reason is, if some astronomical disaster were sure to happen in a year's time—a wandering planet about to throw us for a loop, say—we could speed up so that generations of researchers could develop solutions in time."

Irène had slid the goose into the oven. She stood near the sink beside Gaétan, the heels of her hands gently against the counter's edge. Face toward the window, eyes slipping and caroming off the rims of her spectacles, she said, "Nothing's faster than that April light though." She said it with some satisfaction.

"Incidentally," said Gaétan, "do you and Chantal ever..."

"Make love? We never have. It might have happened in the beginning, I suppose, but it didn't and it seems to me that now the chances against it are astronomical. Jean-Luc and Mouse never have either. Nor Mouse and Chantal. Nor Jean-Luc and I for a long time. Do you think some crossings-over might have helped?"

"Good heavens, who am I to say? Conceivably though—like an electric short, you know." Indeed, early on Irène had rather pushed and schemed for Mouse and Jean-Luc to make love. Once, by coercing promises separately from each, she had managed to make them spend a night in the same bed. This was before Chantal's advent. Irène herself had tactfully slept downstairs to be out of earshot. Her imagination in high gear, she had lain on the sofa with quiet music for a long time wide-eyed in the dark, eventually providing herself with multiple superb orgasms before she drifted off. Apparently nothing so gratifying transpired above. In the morning they had both looked as if they hadn't slept a wink, as was the case, yet also resentful, as they proved to be when Irène had contrived to be alone with Jean-Luc and then Mouse and, dropping the incurious air she had assumed through breakfast, had questioned each. They had given reports so nearly identical that Irène would have suspected them had not the (also nearly identical) strained manner in which they answered her questions been all too authentic. With considerable annoyance each had explained that they had agreed that, having promised to humor her, they might as well climb into the same bed and sleep. They had climbed into bed, turned out the light and tried to sleep, unsuccessfully and without another word all night, in their underclothes, each resolving never again to humor Irène, to go along with no future whim of hers. Irène had been disappointed, almost angry with them but soon she had shrugged it off and forgotten it. But once afterwards in the back kitchen where the washing machine was she was doing the house's laundry and something prompted her to hold to her face a melange of shirts and underclothing of Jean-Luc's and Mouse's, and the smells of their bodies mixing had assured her that it was something that ought to have happened nevertheless. Gaétan said, "Are you ever homesick? I am sometimes, even in Amsterdam."

"Rarely," said Irène. "In the beginning yes, violently."

"Have you and Jean-Luc become U.S. citizens?"

"Legally you mean? No. Our taxes would be the same, I think. The privilege of casting our two votes hardly seems worth the trouble. Reporting our whereabouts annually is a minor annoyance. In fact the government probably monitors the vast majority of its citizens more closely than it monitors us. Because they do cast votes."

"I don't see how you've stuck it out here so long though, Irène. I don't entirely see why either."

"Me neither. One thing though: I don't write the people off. They're good and many of their traditions are very good. My heart goes out to them, Gaé, and so should yours—especially to the younger ones who've spent their whole lives in a regime of ever-increasing manipulativeness, who may have difficulty imagining anything else. But what you said last night was true: they do seem somehow dazed. But I don't think the condition's irreversible. Of course it's not! And they aren't afraid, you see—only naive and dazed. You on the outside oughtn't discount them yet. I refuse to discount the people of Russia, in fact people anywhere. I can't, won't write us off. Not yet. I actually believe a fair good world is possible."

Gaétan laughed. "Hopefulness like that is dangerous, Irène. You'll call the wrath of CIA gods down on your naked head."

"Let's hope they were napping," she said. "They nap, same as you and me. You're not in their employ, by the way, are you?"

"Not to my knowledge. Are you an agent provocateur?"

Irène laughed. "Not to my knowledge either."

III

OUTSIDE UNDER the black walnut tree Mouse watched a white sportscar with its top down cross the stream and climb to the house where it stopped and out hopped Mathurin Kirkwood. This Mathurin's panic fear of aging had most recently manifested itself in a crash diet because of which he now looked unhealthy. Of mixed French and U.S. parentage, Mathurin had spent most of his first twenty years in France and most of the second twenty in Virginia. Long before Jean-Luc's association with the university Mathurin had settled into a rank below Jean-Luc's; he was happy to be tolerated as a sort of decorative fixture. He taught introductions to the French language, never literature. He skied winters, played tennis summers and wheeled young ladies across the floors at balls in all seasons, but his knees weren't strong, it showed in his gait. He bounced from his little car and said, "Mouse, how beautiful you are under that tree! I've been at a horsy do in your neighborhood—deadly, I must be a masochist—and when I thought of how near this house was, I bolted. But I'm sure I'm about to discover that you're all about to set off to Washington for something more interesting than reviving me."

Mouse wouldn't have minded chatting a while there but since she saw that the cooling breezes made Mathurin shiver she led him inside. Irène and Gaétan were talking in the kitchen. Mouse left Mathurin with them and went up to her room. She shut the door quietly behind her and locked it.

In her dark patience she saw her room with a stranger's eyes as a Goodwill store with price tags attached to the seashells, the oriental rugs, the pre-Columbian pottery, the magazine illustrations and maps and drawings on the wall, the old radio, to every moveable thing, smaller numbers on the tags attached to the magazine illustrations and seashells, larger ones on the tags attached to the escritoire and rugs.

With other strangers' eyes she saw her room as behind plexiglass at the Smithsonian Museum, an awkward mockup of Mouse seated at the escritoire. Then for a moment she saw her room with still other eyes as a weapon contrived by a cruel man to hurt her.

Such ways of seeing came to her involuntarily on occasion without alarming her. It was like pain: she could bear it because she knew it would pass, as it did now.

She sat at her escritoire, selected a ballpoint pen and a sheet of paper and began to draw a picture whose deliberate unbroken outlines she would fill tomorrow or the day after with opaque tempera colors. The picture was of six frogs at a dinner table, dressed and coifed as the six people had been the previous night. She drew a corner of paper sticking out of the hip pocket of the dungarees worn by the frog representing herself. She gave the Gaétan frog a broad smile. When the drawing was done she wrote a letter to her parents, telling some anecdotes of life in Virginia sure to amuse them, describing the weather, wishing them well and saying she hoped it would be possible to visit them soon. She added in a postscript that she was writing them because it was her birthday, but that she had them on her mind every day. In a second postscript she added that she had met a few Native Americans—she had learned the term recently and lest her parents not understand she explained with a parenthesis, "(Indians)"—in the U.S. and had read some articles in newspapers, and that as far as she could see Native Americans were getting an even rawer deal from the U.S. government than from the Canadian, but that the next time she wrote she would tell some reasons she had discovered for hope. "Respectfully, Otsinowa." Pleased, she sealed the letter into an envelope.

She stood, slid the chair back into place and stretched in a straight line from wrist to wrist, hands raised, ear against shoulder. Soon her birthday party.

What should Mouse's party garb be? The buckskin squaw clothes she first met Irène in. She undressed and donned them. She braided her hair and placed a large white feather (a gull's feather she had found in Rock Creek Park in Washington) upright at the back of her head— more a brave's than a woman's ornament, but no one at the party would know that. She considered herself in a mirror, not posing and expressionless. In itself her appearance satisfied her but she decided to choose another costume for the party. She took off the squaw clothes, laid them in a drawer and went to her deep closet. She had removed the feather from her hair and held it loosely in her hand. On the threshold she browsed through clothing on hangers, the last April light all down the naked back of her, the feather's edge against her leg at the knee, Mouse thought nothing of how exciting she was, how much she could have asked from anyone just then.

The work that hung over Chantal this weekend was to read further into *The Romance of the Rose* and to finish an essay on *The Charterhouse of Parma*. Her longhand copy of the essay lay on her desk, to be typed tomorrow. While Brad and his friends were below she had done the final revisions and before they left she had propped herself up with pillows on the bed and begun to read. Chantal admired the first part of the poem and was thankful for its lucid comeliness, but she found that she preferred, admired more and felt more thankful for de Meun's exasperating continuation. Her tolerance was low enough that she had put aside the book and was coming to terms with the mere two hundred lines she had read when Jean-Luc entered to tell her about the young citizens' visit and by and by to make movements toward getting a little something started, nuzzling his face up between her thighs.

They had looked out to see who it was when they heard Mathurin's car. "I should say hello," Jean-Luc had said, but now standing by the desk he was glancing over Chantal's essay. It was good. She bogged herself down at points making fruitless distinctions and countering views of the man who taught the course the essay was for, but it was pretty good. It was called, "Time in the Prison House of Narration," and opened with the question, "What are we to make of the unwelcome fact that Stendhal spent less than three months writing *Le Chartreuse de Parme*?"

Chantal said, "Well?"

"Not bad... not that bad at all." They talked for a minute about the essay easily, freely, Jean-Luc giving no more thought to Chantal's self-esteem than he would have done with one of his colleagues (less, in fact) and Chantal receptive, alert, and free (she trusted his judgment far more than he supposed). "I think he'll appreciate it. So. I should go down and say hello to Mathurin, I guess."

"Okay. What time is it?"

"It's . . . my god, it's almost six-thirty. People are invited for seven. Oh well. What are you giving Mouse, by the way?"

"Let it surprise you. Nothing she'll be wild about, I'm afraid. You?"

"I wasn't born yesterday," said Jean-Luc. "See you."

He found Claude, Mathurin and Irène chatting in the kitchen. Irène said that she had to make herself look like a hostess, with a glance to Jean-Luc that meant *Mathurin's as much your responsibility as mine, so you can damn well stay in evidence long enough for me to dress*, and went up. Mathurin was telling Claude things to see and do in the area; when he and Jean-Luc had greeted one another he continued. "You might have a look at the grounds of the University there too. The oldest part is at the center. The same Jefferson designed it. In the courtyard are statues of Washington, Jefferson and Homer. Washington and Jefferson are looking at each other but Homer's blind eyes are on neither. Anyway the colonnade and buildings that bound the courtyard can be affecting. The style is 'federal.' Sort of primly humane, you know?"

Claude said, "You make it sound like lots of Amsterdam."

"It's not, though. The feeling is several shades primmer and perhaps just a shade less humane. Wouldn't you say, Jean-Luc. So if I've managed to tempt you to see the academy you might also want to take a spin through the town. Some of the black neighborhoods might interest you. Extreme poverty, you know. It's in curious pockets strewn about the town, enough off main thoroughfares that one might live there indefinitely without coming upon one. In fact—when was it?—a year or so ago a sort of shack was moved out of one of those pockets by some well-intentioned group and exhibited in the parking lot of a shopping center for several weeks. Do you remember, Jean-Luc?"

"Indeed. Everything about it was . . . uncanny, parents giving tidy explanations to children who'd wondered what the thing was. . . ." Jean-Luc shook his head. "So, Claude, we could drive down there tomorrow if you and Gaétan would like. Except you know, Mathurin, Washington's as near."

"But Washington's the sort of place they'll have other chances to see. But do both. Or haven't they the time?"

"Time?" said Jean-Luc, "I . . ." He was interrupted by laughter from the hallway. It was Mouse and Gaétan. Jean-Luc performed introductions and then in the flurry of talk he slipped away to shave and have a quick shower. He found Irène in the bathroom. As he undressed she completed her evening maquillage, replaced her spectacles and combed her hair. "I didn't hear Mathurin leave," she said.

"Good," said Jean-Luc, "because he's still here. I think Mouse is inviting him to stay for the party."

In the mirror Irène and Jean-Luc looked at each other. Jean-Luc had turned on the shower, the room was filling with steam. The mirror was clouding over. Irène turned, Jean-Luc stood still. Jean-Luc smiled, Irène's spectacles were starting to mist over. He stepped off the fluffy mat onto the cold tiles, came to her, slid his arms around her and she slid hers around him. Feet between feet, from knee to shoulder they pressed and held themselves together strongly, cheek hard against cheek. Until as at a signal they eased the pressure and gave each other a light kiss that said *you never know, do you?* Then Jean-Luc was under the shower spray sudsing his hair and Irène was clip-clopping down the stairwell.

She found Mouse, Gaétan, Claude, and Mathurin sipping cocktails in the long living room, where soft lights had been turned on. Mouse had indeed invited Mathurin to stay on for the party. Gaétan, having caught the end of Mathurin's travelogue, had asked if there were any notable student unrest at the university, and Mathurin was explaining that the students there weren't really the sort to indulge themselves in demonstrations. The tone had begun to change a bit in the past three or four years, since some women students had been admitted. Many of the young men had long hair now and coats and ties were no longer required classroom attire, but basically one still had the impression of being in the 1890s at Harrow or Eton.

Claude had changed into slightly more formal clothes and so had Gaétan, but it didn't matter what he wore, it all somehow looked equally rumpled, seedy and absurd. Mathurin was smooth—with him too one hardly noticed what he wore because invariably he looked as if he had stepped out of an advertisement for costly goods or services in a magazine. Irène's hair shone, she wore a black turtleneck jersey, a long grey felt skirt with a wide alligator belt, dark hose and low black slingback shoes. Mouse's costume was the most exceptional. She wore delicate medium-heeled sandals, transparent hose, a short crocheted skirt a light eggshell lighter than her skin, and a gauzy shirt with a large blurred flower print in taupe and peach and lilac through which occasionally her thin arms and her little breasts were visible. Her unbraided hair fell over her shoulders. She was chic and ungainly and Mathurin had lost his composure for a moment, his heart had skipped a beat when she appeared laughing with Gaétan.

Irène determined that the wherewithal for cocktails was available, adjusted the volume of the sound system to near-inaudible, slipped in a cassette and flicked a switch to PLAY, and went to the kitchen. Immediately there was a knock. Mouse hastened to the door and opened it on a nervous man who was wringing his hands, bobbing, scraping and saying, "hello hello hello" in a voice like an oboe. It was one of Jean-Luc's colleagues, in fact it was the chairman of the French department himself, Mr. Clusel. "Hello," said Mouse, "please come in."

Bustling and jerking, Clusel complied. "Thanks thanks thanks, yes, don't believe I've had the pleasure, no. I see Mathurin's here—hello hello Mathurin, good to see you, good to see you—good, lovely," he brayed. "Léonie (my wife) sends her regrets, you know she had a bit of a tumble from her horse yesterday—nothing broken, happily, only a few muscles pulled, but it looks as if she'll have to keep to her bed for a few days. She's chafing at the bit already, you know—she's so damned active and she does enjoy Jean-Luc and Irène so, she was crushed not to be able to come along, she was seeking solace in a pitcher of martinis when

I toddled off, the children are seeing to dinner, ha ha, I expect it'll be pretty rudimentary, Spartan fare. Well! My my my this house surpasses all I've heard about it, what a marvelous location. Where are Jean-Luc and Irène? Don't tell me they're polishing the silver! Am I early?"

He was a trifle early but the fact was successfully passed over in the forty-five minutes before the other guests arrived. Jean-Luc came down and he and Clusel, drinks in hand, took a turn outdoors in the twilight. The last to come down was Chantal. When she sidled in without a smile on her small flat face, wearing a short brown suede patchwork skirt and an acid green short-sleeved ribbed sweater, with sheer pantyhose, dark smudges on her eye-lids and an old ivory bracelet on her fine wrist, Mathurin's heart skipped another beat, and the party was under way.

Besides Clusel and his absent wife Jean-Luc had invited two other couples whose male halves were colleagues of his. They arrived almost simultaneously around seven-fifteen: Gibbon and Elsa Sweetser and then Blaise and Sally Duclos. Gibbon Sweetser, whose academic prestige was greater than anyone else's in the department, was an unsavory man in whom certain kinds of peculiarly academic self-congratulation and meanness of spirit had hypertrophied. His wife was more gracious and intelligent. Jean-Luc had invited them in payment of an overdue social debt. Blaise and Sally on the other hand were friends of a sort, and genuinely welcome. Blaise's academic status was like Jean-Luc's and they were coevals. Blaise was pleasant, imperturbable and not unattractive. His wife Sally was the freckled New Yorker with whom Jean-Luc had had an affair shortly before he fell in love with Chantal. Chantal's essay on *The Charterhouse of Parma* was for Blaise's Stendhal seminar.

The predictable began to occur. Academics clustered and talked shop, others clumped and talked of their interests. Mathurin didn't clump, but flirted in his way with Chantal and Mouse. Irène and Jean-Luc circulated with hors d'oeuvres and freshened drinks and with Gaétan and Claude, bringing them now to the wives, now to the professors. Paper safety matches ignited, blue-white figures rose from ends of cigarettes and mushroomed, mouths formed *u* and plumes like frosty steam angled out from them. There was gentle laughter, fulsome laughter, courteous token laughter, clinking of ice, wit, smiling nods of understanding, wanness, sheen, thoughtfulness before speech or after, anecdotes. Jean-Luc had never spoken of either Sally or Chantal to the other. Sally immediately perceived that Jean-Luc and Chantal were lovers; Chantal soon wondered whether Sally and Jean-Luc had been lovers. Gibbon's greedy curiosity was beside itself: *Does Jean-Luc keep a harem? Who sleeps where?* Irène had made the puff-pastry herself—what an extravagance! The gasoline shortage was apparently more of a grief in France than here. Apparently four U.S. corporations had been formulating U.S. government policies for the Middle East since the fifties. The new skyscraper in Paris should never have been built in Paris, it should be dismantled and moved into the suburbs. Picasso dead, was it possible? Were Tunisia and Libya merging or not? How many dictatorships was the U.S. going to be able to underwrite, and for how long? Wasn't it beginning to overextend itself now with Chile? What would one do if it came apart at the seams? Josephine Baker appearing in New York—how old must she be? The new Japanese pocket calculators were delightful. One sometimes found locally-grown vegetables at roadside stands. Charlottesville skies were varied and—remember the New Year's Eve sunset two or three years ago? Some California wines were adequate but the cost was outrageous and there was no way of knowing what chemicals might have gone into them. Cancer might become as common in France as here, if U.S. food industries ever succeeded there, god forbid. Vionnet's bias cutting, dear Duchamp's last work, apparently one of the more distinguished sex-change surgeons was at the university—people came from all over the world, it seemed. The university had a parapsychology division too. Amsterdam ought to be interesting. You have a curious accent and you look like an American Indian. I don't believe I've ever met one before, had you, dear? You mean that's actually your name and not a nickname. Apparently you're a very extraordinary student, your praises are sung widely. When was it we were here last? Irène's looking marvelous. Wonder if Duchamp ever wrote music.

As it will, the unpredictable was also occurring. The guests Irène had invited, Mouse's friends coming for her birthday, were to have arrived around seven, and it was half past eight. How much longer to wait dinner?, Irène wondered. Chantal and Blaise were talking of Stendhal and each understood much of what the other said. A car drove up, stopped under the trees with the others, its lights went dark. Irène smiled and patted Gaétan on the shoulder. Car doors slammed and there was the briefest quietness in the conversation. Irène went out onto the lighted porch—her pullover felt good on the tops of her arms and down her back in the cooler outside night. She heard strange giggling under the trees. It wasn't the people she had invited for Mouse. It was Brad, Jeff, Craig, Mimmy and Rosie crunching over the gravel into the light. Mimmy said, "Hi there. Your husband told us to come back and here we are." It was hard to understand.

They had missed some turn or other and gotten completely lost. They had driven for what seemed an eternity on back country roads, asking directions from a farm wife at her mailbox, later from a farmer in his pickup, each time had soon disagreed about the directions, had decided to forget the rock concert, had smoked some dope and drunk some cheap wine beside an unidentified river, had thought they heard a rattlesnake, had re-entered the car and driven more in the dark and miraculously found themselves passing and recognizing (Rosie had recognized it) the entrance to the ordinary's long driveway, and were hungry.

"I think we all are," Jean-Luc told Irène as he shepherded the young wanderers past her into the house. Mouse came out onto the porch. "Funny," she said and then, "By the way, when are Louie and Ninon coming?" Irène said, "Don't know, my girl. I told them seven. We're at least quite sure they knew it was tonight." Mouse smiled. They stood talking for a moment, arms lightly around each other's waists, and had decided there was nothing for it but to begin dinner and were turning, when lights twinkled through the trees on the hill opposite.

The car came down across the stream, up and stopped near the porch, a pink '62 Chevy hardtop convertible. Out one side stepped Mouse's fellow waitress Ninon, a pale, large-boned woman in a multicolor gossamer pantsuit that ballooned in the breeze, with elaborate blonde hair and amazingly long synthetic lashes affixed to her turquoise lids. "Mouse, Happy Birthday." Out the other side stepped Louie who happened to resemble Louis Armstrong at forty or fifty more than a little. He was natty as could be in a light grey sharkskin suit, dark silk tie and glistening shoes. He spoke no French. "Hey there, Mousie," he said, "and a happy birthday to you. Hey, Irène—everything under control, baby?" When he smiled, his rich skin lightened in creases above his cheeks and at his dimples.

Mouse ran to kiss them both. But there was someone else in the car too, in the back seat getting out slowly, a large figure. From the porch Irène watched. Mouse stood between Louie and Ninon on the grass. Her eyes widened and kept widening, she clapped her hands over her mouth. It's impossible, she was thinking as out of the car and forward into the light came the extraordinary figure of Grace Coyote herself, short and thickset. Her black eyes were clear and merry, two of her teeth were missing, she had a wide forehead. Her hair hung almost to her elbows, she held the strap of her handbag with both hands in a decorous old-fashioned way, wrists beneath breasts. It was a dowdy black purse with a fluorescent green button on it reading "Impeach" and the name of the current U.S. president. She wore a light green cotton mail-order shirtwaist dress, a black shawl and ankle-high deerskin moccasins. Her skin was like Mouse's dusted over, with many fine wrinkles.

Grace and Mouse had met several years before when

Grace and some other North American Indians were travelling about the continent to establish contacts with widely separated native peoples. The group had visited the reservation in Canada for a week in February when trappers came back snowblind. Grace Coyote had lodged with Mouse's parents and it had been Mouse's good fortune to be there at the time. There had been a sweat lodge ceremony and a social dance, both memorable, but most of the intercourse between visitors and natives had been informal. Mouse's parents afterwards avowed that they'd never had a better guest, and Mouse knew it was true, not only because Grace had fitted perfectly into the routine of things, helping with household chores, watching television, but also because of the way Grace had talked. Mouse had told Irène how much she had learned from Grace Coyote, listening to whatever she said, thinking about it, scarcely believing it was possible as it happened. Mouse had explained to Irène that, little as it was, it had seemed everything. To learn that wonder of wonders it really was true that her blood was in no wise cause for shame. To learn and understand why. It was absurd but it actually was the case that before Grace's visit Mouse had not quite been able to see that the Europeans' treatment of her people had been a joke from the word go and was still shameful and like children's behavior. Telling Irène about it, Mouse had laughed at herself for having had such simple things to learn. Irène had shook her head. "Those things are hard to learn and hard to remember too. I don't know why."

As Mouse's birthday approached Irène on a long shot had spent the better part of a day in Washington newspaper morgues and phone booths, truant from her own work.

When she finally reached Grace in Nevada, the long shot had paid off: Grace was on her way to Washington and would be very pleased to come to the party for Mouse whom she remembered well. So it was that in the sweet Virginia April night air Grace Coyote appeared to Mouse's wondering eyes.

"What's happening?" called Jean-Luc from the door.

As they went in, Louie apologized for being late. His pink Chevy had broken down on a lonely stretch of the highway and he'd feared for his life. "A black man down here, with two women, one white and the other not exactly black? You people can't imagine. This your old man, Irène? Pleased to meet you." Ninon had said, "Oh, Mouse, let me tell you what happened at the crêperie! You wouldn't believe it," in a stage whisper and, clutching Mouse's arm, was recounting an episode that had left her breathless. Grace was explaining to Irène that it was she rather than Louie who had diagnosed and corrected the malfunction in the car's engine.

There was no single moment when the movement of recession began. The occupants of the ordinary already were withholding some assent and it was happening complexly and by degrees in innumerable moments over their whole time there, and during their earlier lives too, as perhaps all decisions of that order of difficulty and of that gravity are made. But if things had been simpler, if any single moment had been the actual beginning, it would have been when Mouse, Irène and Jean-Luc brought Louie, Ninon and Grace Coyote into the living room. Jean-Luc hadn't quite prepared the professors and spouses, nor had anyone else. Jean-Luc had been getting around to it when Brad and his friends came, and their appearance had to be explained and accounted for. Easing and smoothing over that shock with all his charm, Jean-Luc had let the greater shock that was imminent slip his mind until it was too late and then, coming back inside with the others, had told himself that it was all simply too preposterous to be concerned about, things would work themselves out, had to. The six came through the doorway, fanned out into a crescent and then came to a stop just over the threshold because the volume of talk and laughter in the room was plummeting. Mr. Clusel brayed on in a solo, "Oh yes oh yes oh yes yes yes," until he too heard the silence and turned to peer. In that brief silence Chantal near the sofa and Jean-Luc, Irène and Mouse in the arrested crescent happened to glance into one another's eyes and realize that they all understood and evaluated the fleeting silence alike together. No more than that, and they were almost immediately to forget it, none happening to recall it later gave it much thought and when any of them spoke of the moment afterwards it was to laugh about the sudden silence, the surprise on the students' faces, the bafflement or consternation showing through smiles of a moment before that had stayed awkwardly on the faces of professors and wives. So that they never happened later to speak of the intelligence flashing among the four of them by virtue of which the moment would be the beginning of freedom itself were that beginning locatable in any moment.

 The little silence was over almost before it began. Unprecedented as it was to find oneself invited to dine with such outlandish specimens as Ninon, Grace Coyote and Louie, incomprehensible as were Jean-Luc's and Irène's motives in arranging it, disagreeable or difficult as the evening seemed likely to prove, it was still immediately clear that these people had been expected. The volume of talk rebounded. "Far out," said Rosie to Mimmy. Gibbon Sweetser said, "Hired performers of some sort, how novel," into his wife Elsa's ear. Chantal as fourth host came forward to welcome the new guests. Irène went off to the kitchen.

 Now that there was an explanation for the prolongation of the cocktail hour it could go on a bit further with more drinks, smoke, laughter and talk, people circulating and migrating about the large room. Mouse detached herself from Ninon (whom she left ogling Jean-Luc) and sat beside Grace on the sofa. Chantal brought more hors d'oeuvres and moved from group to group offering them. Irène with her social smile led Louie past the younger people and Claude and Gaétan to the corner where most of Jean-Luc's colleagues and their wives had stationed themselves, and introduced him. Save Sally, herself a New Yorker, they were sometimes unable to follow Louie's Harlem English, and Louie for his part sometimes mistakenly suspected the motives behind an excessively formal turn of phrase of theirs, but a conversation of sorts did ensue about ways of acquiring money, theirs and his. Louie had boxed professionally in his youth but since then had managed to scare up such money as he needed without benefit of a profession. At last Jean-Luc summoned everyone to dinner. Cigarettes were stubbed out, glasses drained. People chose places around the five tables shoved together to make a rough oval and when the jostling subsided language seemed the only absolute criterion for seating: those who spoke only English were contiguous; otherwise the several groups had interlaced.

It was a long and excellent meal, and some were impressed by the series of courses that had resulted from combining the menus planned for successive evenings: Irène's crudités, Jean-Luc's steak au poivre, Irène's roast duck, Jean-Luc's cheeses and Irène's cherry and maple-sugar tarte, with appropriate wines. Irène's dishes were approximations of Iroquois cuisine. The fact prompted discussions of other regional Indian cuisines and it was agreed that perhaps in New York and certainly in Paris an American Indian restaurant ought to do well. Jean-Luc and Sally, side by side, were able to catch up, find how things had gone since they were intimate. Across the table Mouse and Grace Coyote were similarly absorbed. Because Grace knew almost no French they had to use English, in which Grace was far more fluent and correct than Mouse, having been forced to learn it well in a California government school for Indian children in the twenties, when the policy of punishing children caught using their own tongues was in force. Other dinner partners talked of other things—Elsa Sweetser and Claude discovered they had common friends in Brussels—and there was an almost continual din, even though much of the noise and heat escaped through open windows and doors. Twice, though, in brief lulls, things were said that almost everyone listened to. Gibbon Sweetser leaned forward with his weak bright eyes and said, "Begging your pardon, Miss Coyote: I wonder if you could tell us something about your national literature. I myself confess rank ignorance of it." Across the table Grace said, "National literature? Do you mean famous stories and songs? Well there are many we admire and love. Lots of them are very comical." Later in the meal Irène speaking of Jean-Luc to Blaise at her side grew vehement and, when she realized that nearly everyone at the table was listening, continued quite as though Blaise alone heard, and delivered herself of a fairly impassioned testimonial to her husband's knowledge of French letters. It was an uncharacteristic sort of thing for her to do—it was more in Jean-Luc's line, and even he probably wouldn't have done it before so large an audience—so that there followed an awkward silence which might have ended still more awkwardly had not Mr. Clusel's blaring "Hear, hear!" absolved everyone, and the din recommenced. Course followed delicious course with surprising speed, much wine was drunk, coffee with the tarte and more after.

Mr. Clusel departed in a gale of thanks. The Sweetsers departed. Sally and Blaise conferred, Jean-Luc urged them not to go yet, they wanted not to but their sitter had to be released. Sally would go, Blaise could ride back with Mathurin. At the door Sally with a twinkle in her eye told Jean-Luc, "The little Chantal is a pretty foxy number. Good night, Jean-Luc, it was fun. Don't let Blaise drink too much of your good scotch." The meal was over and people were drifting into the living room with coffee and cigarettes.

Gaétan asked Mouse to introduce him to Ninon. Mouse impassive, dark eyes lowered, and Gaétan attentive and eager basked in Ninon's silvery craziness in the center of the room. Ninon offered soft rushes of words and breathy menthol smoke, sipped a sparkling dessert wine, explored the back of her coiffure with fingertips, flicked the top of her pantsuit into a new arrangement over her bosom, lifted high her lashes, lifted them higher, glanced over the room or deeply into Gaétan's and Mouse's eyes, all with the same mild urgent sincerity. She spoke of gelatine capsules, Shasta lo-cal ginger ale, Star Trek and other recent finds of hers, she said that the dinner must have cost a great deal, she found the house charming and in good taste, she was eager to see Mouse's room later, she could hardly believe Jean-Luc was a professor, he was so handsome, and she wondered what the scent he wore was. Gaétan and Mouse were models of decorum.

Jeff, Craig and Rosie had gathered around Grace where she sat on the sofa, her handbag on her knees. She had been explaining that it is a mistake to wreak havoc on our mother the earth. "It's the rich who're making that mistake, right?, with their industries and governments and armies. Well, I think it would be good if they all went to the moon. It costs a lot but they could put their money together and then they all could go there and stay, and leave the earth to us who love her. They don't love her. Maybe they'd like the moon better." The young people had never seen an adult with missing teeth in real life and it was hard for them not to stare at Grace's mouth, especially when she smiled.

Jeff struggled for adequate words for what was in his mind: "Like, like we'd like to know what dignity is. I would anyway, and I tend to look for it in the lives of the poor. There might be real dignity in the lives of the rich too, but with them it's . . . obscured by the trappings of dignity they buy. I don't know but I think my generation's having trouble locating something to admire. I am, anyway." A full black moon swam toward Rosie, Louie's face near hers, his warm hand on her shoulder. "Can I get you to help me bring some presents in?" he said. Far out.

Blaise pushed through a swinging door into the kitchen where Chantal and Irène were readying an ice-cream bombe and birthday cake. Blaise asked if they needed help and, told no with thanks, stayed leaning against a wall to make suave chat and eye the two women. Cool solid Irène and wilful little Chantal, they complemented one another excellently as they worked in the fluorescent light, Blaise thought. With a close intuition of how things stood in the household, he thought better of making advances to Chantal that evening. Furthermore she was his student, his best. Irène, however. . . .

When it was time to open presents with everyone gathered and expectant, Mouse again felt shy. Too much seemed to depend on her. As she unwrapped gift after gift, gratefulness confused her and gave her a diffidence. She wished this part of the party could go quickly but she knew everyone was counting on the pleasure of its unfolding without haste, and she proceeded accordingly, allowing time for each gift to be handed around and admired before she opened the next, the order ostensibly random though in fact she was careful to intersperse her housemates' packages with the others, and to open Irène's neither first nor last. All pleased and some amused her. Only Irène's gift—records, Iroquois songs, Greco—disappointed her, and only because it was from Irène, and less when she reminded herself of Irène's other gifts, the party and Grace Coyote's presence. The rolls of film and photo album from Jean-Luc may have been more disappointing in themselves, but less was at issue there. Chantal's gift, though, was beautiful—an intricate necklace, almost a bib, of a light tinny metal. It had been made in India, there was an Indian boutique in Charlottesville. Gaétan and Claude of course hadn't been able to shop, but they had nevertheless come up with a gift, a black-and-white photo of a narrow street in a part of Los Angeles called Venice, taken early on a hot afternoon when there were many people out. Down at the end of the street one saw a beach with more people and a dog on it, with Pacific Ocean water beyond. It was one of the most crucial of the photos Claude and Gaétan had made in L.A., one of the few they had printed there. And, as Gaétan told Irène later, they were giving it to Mouse completely since its negative had disappeared and this was the sole print. Grace's present was an Inuit soapstone carving and like the photo it was irreplaceable and valued by its donor. With the best and kindest intentions Ninon had chosen an electric hair-curling kit in an embossed pink vinyl overnight case for Mouse. Ninon had one of her own and found it indispensable. Everyone laughed, whistled and applauded when they saw Louie's gift, assorted underclothing from Frederick's of Hollywood.

Then there was music and dancing. Mouse put on her Brazilian dances at a high volume, Irène unobtrusively turned the volume up a little more. Louie and Mouse began the dancing (which others soon joined) and through the early morning hours, as partners changed, as the party swirled into every room of the house, as people fell asleep, made love, talked, ate and drank and smoked tobacco or marijuana, Louie and Mouse danced together repeatedly. In South American dances she taught him, in U.S. black dances he taught her, in the many many dances from the earlier part of the century they both knew—maxixe, cakewalk—in whatever kind of dancing they did, they were easily the best to watch. Irène danced indifferently and didn't especially enjoy it, but the occasion wouldn't have seemed complete without her dancing at least once with Mouse. They did a discreet foxtrot with neither leading or following more than the other, after Grace Coyote had gone to bed. Nor was all the dancing in couples. Before Grace went to bed she and Mouse taught others some Native American group dances, and then sometimes in lively moments when the music was fast and hard there would be trios or people dancing alone among the pairs.

The guests from Washington had meant to return that night and so had those from Charlottesville but, what with the lateness of dinner, the dancing and general festivity, and their hosts' welcoming friendliness, none did. Flirtations and seductions in progress also helped keep them there. These varied widely with the principals involved. The least satisfactory were probably those of Mathurin, who plied every woman but Grace and Irène with lavish urbanity to no avail until toward dawn he went good-humoredly to sleep. That with the most far-reaching consequences was Louie's and Rosie's.

Louie had had eyes for Rosie from the first moment he saw her but, consummate gentleman that he was, and observant and kind, he had held off until late—until after he had seen Mouse cast a quizzical look toward Irène and Blaise (who were deep in conversation) and then led Rosie out of the room up the stair, until Rosie and Mouse had reappeared an hour later (in the interim Irène and

Blaise had disappeared). Only then, when Mouse was dancing with Mathurin, did Louie stroll over to Rosie and ask if she had seen the upstairs. "A little," she said, "let's go see more." They found an unoccupied room with a bed, a radio and soft lights and very soon they were making love. "Wow," breathed Rosie, "wow, wow." "Oooh baby," said Louie, "it's so *good*." It was so good that it lasted until dawn, he invited her to Washington for the next weekend and so began a long love and firm friendship. She was to learn that he had come to Washington because in New York there was a contract out on him. She was to learn much more that would have astonished her had she known it that first night at the ordinary. He had spent five years in prisons and jails in and around New York, and he had a wife and two sons older than Rosie in Brooklyn. He had known many famous jazz musicians in the old days—though here as in other matters he maintained a certain vagueness about details and sometimes, Rosie was to learn, played fast and loose with the truth. He was to discover much about her too, much that had he had an inkling of it the night of Mouse's party he might have foregone his pleasure. She wasn't, for instance, slumming. She had a mind of her own, and a will, he was to see as he came to love her more than he had loved any woman. Their lovemaking was to get better and better, though it seemed good as possible upstairs at the ordinary all the way till dawn, the radio whose station had signed off left to whisper on like an encouragement.

It was Gaétan's and Claude's last night in the country and they were inclined to make the most of it but the exhilaration of foreignness was giving way to thoughts of home and ease. Claude went up first, Gaétan talked with Jean-Luc for another hour. Claude was awake when Gaétan came into their room. He sat on the bed to untie his shoes. "I do wish they'd all come to Amsterdam. But they won't." He finished undressing and slid into bed beside Claude. "Listen, do you feel at all . . ."

"I wouldn't mind," said Claude and then, as they began to make love, "They probably won't, but they might, or some of them. What fun it would be."

"I dread the flight," said Gaétan, "It's going to be worse than coming over."

"We'll probably be tired enough to sleep some," said Claude. "Hey, what are you doing?"

"I'm not quite sure myself, I . . . you know, it really is a waste of time for them to be here. I mean, in Amsterdam. . . ."

"I agree."

"Oh well."

"Mmm. This good?"

"Yes, don't stop."

Downstairs there was still loud music, sporadic dancing, quiet laughter, smoke. Beds had been shown to Grace and Ninon—further assignments were pointless since no one was likely to remember or heed them, but all had been assured that with sofas and foam mattresses all could be accommodated. After Gaétan had said good night, Jean-Luc found Chantal in the back kitchen gently but firmly refusing Mathurin's invitation to dance. Mathurin went away and Jean-Luc and Chantal tried to decide whether as hosts they had to remain in evidence. Though the party was for Mouse she was still in some measure a host and she and Irène seemed to have disappeared for the night. Jean-Luc and Chantal agreed that, though this fact could be seen as increasing their own obligation to remain below until the end of the party, they would see it as removing that obligation entirely. Then separately they went up to their room. When both were there they found that their ruse made them less sleepy. It was like being children pretending to be adults, prowlers of some sort who had entered by a window. Chantal stood at the window gazing out, unzipping her skirt. There was fog on the grass, the cars floated in it. Jean-Luc was unbuttoning his shirt. He had an erection, he pushed against Chantal's buttocks. They finished undressing each other and made silent love deliciously in the window, came soon and then he carried her across the room and they fell onto the bed, finally making a noise that would have alerted light sleepers in a quieter house.

The first perceptible lightening of the darkness outside, an unavoidable reminder of the expenditure of time, prompted the remaining partiers below to find places to sleep. Mathurin in spite of all his efforts was alone, on the sofa. Craig had long since lost consciousness across a low table. Jeff had dozed off waiting for Rosie among jumbles of dishes on the kitchen floor. Mimmy and Brad were the last. By then the sun had risen completely and it was a clear morning. Brad and Mimmy opened the front door and left it open to let fresh air come into the house. Without thinking of turning off the music they went back to Irène's study to undress, smoke another joint and then fall asleep on the daybed there.

"Weird party," said Brad.

"It was okay," Mimmy said. "I saw you were talking to the old Indian woman. I wonder if she really is Indian."

"What else? Listen, did you know that one of the models for our constitution was Indian? She told me about an Iroquois confederation that's still in existence, and that Ben Franklin researched for us."

"You believe it's true?"

"Jeez, Mimmy."

"It's just that she was so weird, you know?"

"I had an interesting conversation with her though. Did you talk to the black dude?"

"No."

"Me neither, but I wish I had. You dance with him?"

"No. He's fantastic though."

"Sure is. But, wow, Mimmy, are we ever going to have to mean business if we're to get all that eco shit memorized in time for the quiz!"

"I forgot to tell you: they postponed it till next week."

"Nice. It'll still be a shitload of memorizing though. Want to do it Thursday night?"

"Sure. Oh no—I've got a three-page art history paper due Friday. Let's do it sometime Sunday."

From seven to nine-thirty, through some twelve repetitions of a recording of hectic songs about violence and despair, not a creature stirred in the house. At nine-thirty the radio in the room with Louie and Rosie, which had gone from soft whispering to mild music at seven without waking them, began to buzz, for it was a clock radio with an alarm Louie had set without knowing it. The radio buzzed until they woke and shut it off, and Rosie decided she ought to go looking for Jeff. She was halfway downstairs when she heard footsteps. It was Louie barefoot and shirtless with his Washington address and phone number and another matchbook for her to write hers on if she felt like it. Rosie did. The exchange made, they embraced and kissed, "Good-bye for now, and see you soon," and as they were doing it became aware that someone had come into the hallway and was watching them. Mrs. Spotswood, the owner of the ordinary, had come to pay a call on her tenants.

The night before in a table-rapping session with friends Mrs. Spotswood's husband had informed her that since his death he had thought of no one but her. She was cheered and flattered. When she woke in the morning she had felt the urge to vent her good spirits in an act of graciousness. A call on the young French couple in the ordinary would be perfect. She remembered them as polite, and it might be that during the visit over tea she would confide the news about her husband. The number of cars made her suppose that an early brunch was in progress. What a sweet house it was!—though the boxwood did need a trimming. The music seemed inappropriate and the open front door puzzled her. She rapped against it brightly, rapped again. When there was still no answer she ventured into the dim hallway where she was startled by what she saw ahead through the doorway that gave onto the kitchen: unconscionable disorder and a motionless youth sprawled on the floor. Mrs. Spotswood turned quickly and had gone some way into the loud living room before she realized that in spite of the music there was no movement here either except hers, which ceased abruptly because here too was disorder and people in the most abandoned postures. Mrs. Spotswood raised her hand to her throat. Explanations and excuses for this enormity sped through her mind, all so inadequate that she rejected not only them but also everything she had seen and, hearing steps and voices in the hallway, whirled and went there with a girlish smile, like a hostess at a lovely garden party who must break off conversation with one distinguished gentleman to welcome the still more distinguished, possibly titled, guest of honor. Only to undergo a crueller shock. It was Louie and Rosie. Mrs. Spotswood was more open-minded than most of her friends; the motives behind most of her unexamined life were generally good; she knew the times were changing. But she had never seen a black man kiss a white woman. And he was half-naked, and she was practically a child. And the house was a shambles with bodies strewn about it, and the music was tasteless and loud, and it was nine-thirty or ten in the morning, a Sunday. Mrs. Spotswood needed help—she could not imagine what would be proper for her to do in the situation. "Hi," said Rosie.

Luckily at that moment Gaétan appeared and took charge. He recognized Mrs. Spotswood at once as a kind of person he had often dealt with, he saw what the situation was, and knew it would worsen if Rosie or Louie were allowed to say more. "Please come this way," he said, hoping she knew no French and would be the more confused and docile as he led her firmly out onto the porch and closed the door behind. He was fully if rather oddly dressed and he seemed civilized. French was assumed to be one of Mrs.

Spotswood's accomplishments; in fact she had once had a passing acquaintance with it. She was still able to recognize the sound of the language; Gaétan's meaning eluded her. In English she explained who she was and why she was there (though she made no mention of the table-rapping). Gaétan at his courtliest and most soothing led her down the steps and strolled around the black walnut tree with her. In broken English he hoped would amuse her he did his best to make light of the state of affairs inside and to absolve the tenants. He professed shock even greater than Mrs. Spotswood's and then laughed at himself for having concerned himself so with so transitory and inconsequential a turn of events, one that Jean-Luc, Irène, Mouse and Chantal, who had been still more appalled than he, would hereafter take perhaps excessive pains to avoid the most attenuated repetition of. Adding that the four of them were at the moment closeted to determine that means compatible with at least an appearance of restraint by which they could clear the house quickest, and that in kindness to them he wouldn't burden them with the fact that she had happened by, he led her to her car, helped her into it and waved as she drove off.

As it happened the assorted Washington and Charlottesville guests did leave soon, of their own accord. When Gaétan went inside he shut off the record player, and the sudden onset of quiet woke most of the sleepers. Mouse, all puffy-eyed, came down to brew coffee for them and help locate their wraps and other belongings. It was hard for her to say good-bye to Grace. "I hope we can keep in touch," she said. "We can," said Grace, laughing at Mouse's wistfulness. She sat in the back seat of Louie's pink car with an air of great satisfaction and expectancy, like someone embarking on a pleasure-cruise, with her purse balanced on her knees. Out the window she told Brad and his friends, "You're all welcome here. Let us know if there's anything we can do to make your stay more comfortable," and then she said, "Right, Mouse?"

Mouse climbed into bed with Irène and snuggled against her. "Hi."

"What? Oh." Irène turned over and kissed Mouse.

"They've all gone. A broad who looks like some of my customers at the crêperie came and talked to Gaétan. She's gone too. You have a hangover."

"Ouf, why do we do it to ourselves?"

"You fucked Blaise last night. Tell the truth. It matters not a whit."

"I don't think I really meant to."

Mouse sighed.

Irène said, "Remember, Sally his wife had been Jean-Luc's floozie, so there was that added fillip. We were in my study and I was more curious than anything else. About how so polished and diffident a flirter would proceed. Well! You can't imagine, Mouse. All of a sudden, just like that, he was all over me like a monkey. More rape than lovemaking. And then when it was over, snap, from monkey to raffiné."

"Did you enjoy it?"

"I can't remember. I don't think so. But my curiosity was more than satisfied. Are you angry?"

"I'm not."

"Wise, because . . ."

"I was going to tell you anyway."

"Her name's Rosie, no? And you've fallen in love with her."

"Don't be silly, Irène."

"Okay. Tell me about it." Irène put her arm around Mouse's waist and rubbed her feet against Mouse's.

After a moment's reflection Mouse said, "It wasn't bad. She'd never made love with a woman before. But I liked it. She didn't ask boring questions afterwards either. I didn't fall in love with her, yet I could have and you could too. And I believe Louie did, the rascal."

Irène's cheek lay on Mouse's hair. "Can we sleep some more?"

"Sure." Mouse freed her hair, kissed Irène and turned over, still snuggling. They slept.

Gaétan and Claude boarded their plane and were gone, most of the dishes from the weekend were washed and re-soiled by the next weekend. There were no more parties and many fewer guests at the house in the woods through that spring and until the first of July when new tenants threw a housewarming bash. The rest of April, May and June was like an interregnum there. White on rough black, the dogwood looked contrived and Japanese however one arranged it, but not so the bouquets of weaker wildflowers. It was a period of latitude and gentleness, of uncertainty. A mockingbird in the near thicket called hours on end in the soft evening air. There were angry quarrels between Jean-

Luc and Irène but they were less frequent and over sooner, never quite resolved but shelved as by a spontaneous shared decision, as if the quarrelling were a garment one found not quite right for the occasion or the weather whenever one slipped into it. Jean-Luc's and Chantal's one or two brief quarrels were similar, and Irène and Mouse were calm with one another. As for the less intimate relations, the tone of the continuing reserve changed. When Jean-Luc came down for a beer to grade five more essays with before he slept, and Mouse was ironing the coif she wore at work, and no words passed, when Chantal or Irène had misplaced a book, a piece of jewelry, and the other recalled having seen it and provided the information in few words without eye contact, it was not so much with edgy caution as before, but rather out of a kind of unsure delicacy. The time felt uneventful though it was not. Chantal was awakened by abdominal pain proof against the remedies she knew, so much worse by morning that she went to the university hospital instead of her class with Blaise. It was appendicitis and the operation was performed that afternoon. There were no complications and the convalescence was short; still she had missed so many classes that she chose to apply for extensions, and took all her final exams in mid-June. Such events occurred no less often than before and yet it seemed as if they were no more than surface lights, as if a stillness and a waiting underlay them. When Jean-Luc read a detective novel, when Irène and Mouse dined in Washington at the little restaurant where they'd dined the day of their meeting (and had the same waiter, who remembered them, remembered the war paint Mouse had worn but made no allusion to it), when Chantal and

Jean-Luc made love upon waking, when Irène washed her face and without drying it put on her wide spectacles and regarded herself in the mirror, when the four of them after dinner tried to solve a crossword puzzle in English, it was as if it didn't matter because whatever they did was a pastime. Nothing seemed momentous and yet the time seemed momentous. There were clear days, rainy days, wasps in the attic, fog almost every night. The first Russian since Trotsky to have citizenship revoked was Solzhenitsyn. In China there were condemnations of Confucius and Beethoven. Gasoline was a problem. Any number of times a day Irène would decide to quit smoking. There was famine in Ethiopia and elsewhere. True, but whatever you happened to read in the newspapers during that time seemed muted, partly because you didn't talk about it or much think about it either. Not that you took refuge in some kind of ignorance or dismissal. Not at all—what occurred occurred and you took cognizance of it and weighed and remembered. All the more for the lull ambient in the ordinary. And let the new grass burgeon down the hillside, mud dauber wasps lay their tubes, doves putter in the gravel, coffee grounds as they cooled and perished in a grocery bag stain the late air with sequences of a hundred stains, you never supposed these things were other than contingent or even that they were somehow your due. And certainly not that the peacefulness in which they were noted was itself any kind of security against vileness and devastation. Such delusions could be dispensed with. It was as if all bets were off about yourselves, about everything, and the most important thing was to take note, watch how the minutes and hours passed because they seemed precious. Two days after her birthday Mouse was gathering clothes to wash and as she emptied pockets she came upon the slip of paper in the hip pocket of her jeans, the one she'd secretly felt of at dinner the night before the party. It was a jeweler's receipt for the extravagant sum Irène had paid for the gold watch she had given Jean-Luc for his birthday some months before. Mouse crumpled it and dropped it into her wastebasket. She had somehow known that Irène's corresponding gift to her would be far cheaper; she had expected to have to confront Irène with proof of the inequity; now it seemed pointless. Mouse knew what she knew and would do what she had to. She would do what was right and good insofar as she could but, at least for the time, it was worse than futile to talk about prices of gifts. Once she saw a fox, and there was a red-tailed hawk that patrolled the area. On one hilltop a day or two after a rain there would be shoots of wild asparagus. Night trips back from Washington or Charlottesville headlights froze deer, rabbits, slow opossums. There were more and more crayfish in the stream and raccoons came to dine on them. One Saturday Jean-Luc made definite progress with Molière. The course of one dinner was altered by a short circuit in the stove which blew a fuse in the cellar.

In May when a notice to vacate came there was remarkably little interest in it. Gaétan's masterly handling of Mrs. Spotswood had sufficed to postpone the blow but not to deflect it. There was no way he could have known that Mrs. Spotswood didn't know that in addition to the French couple there were two young women residing in the house. It was irregular, increasingly so as the effect of Gaétan's charm wore off and as (though she received no direct communication about it) she considered what Mr. Spotswood would have done, until she instructed her secretary to replace the house's occupants. The outgoing occupants agreed that it was infuriating, with amusement and no trace of fury in their looks and voices. It was as if Mrs. Spotswood's decision lay outside their realm of consequence and practicality, as if it had been offered for their entertainment and they were not disposed to dwell on its deficiencies.

They had begun haphazard inquiries at realty agencies and desultory perusals of classified ads in newspapers when out of the blue came an offer for Jean-Luc to teach at Laval University in the city of Québec for two years starting in September. Jean-Luc relayed the information one night at dinner in an offhand way. It was received similarly, a change of scene was discussed lightly, and then the talk moved on to other topics. The possibility of a move to Canada hadn't quite been denied, though. For several days there was no mention of it, and then when it arose again it was clear that each of the four had come to take it seriously. What the move might entail was discussed again, still playfully but less fancifully. That night Irène wrote her editor asking whether she might be transferred. The next day Chantal investigated procedures for transferring Virginia course credits. The next Monday Mouse went for a long walk in the woods. She sat on a stone in the sun and watched white butterflies dance over shallow water.

These four lived in Québec for five years, through the waning separatism of that time and the end of the U.S. involvement in southeast Asia. They lived together in a small house on a cul-de-sac in the lower town for three of the years and then Irène and Mouse moved to an apartment in the newer suburbs. Jean-Luc's two-year contract at Laval was renewed once, and then once more. Five years in that city proved enough for Mouse and Irène, who separated for nearly a year, Mouse living with old friends and family members on her reservation, Irène in Paris or Toulon, and sometimes in the Near East, still writing for *Le Monde*. Jean-Luc and Chantal felt a little superior to have stayed together, renovating the house, Chantal earning an engineering degree finally, until they too separated, with some rancor prompted by Chantal's having in a sense fallen in love with a fellow student, a die-hard free-Québecer and chain-smoker who talked of the imminent revolution as they lay tangled in his sheets, thrilling Chantal even though she knew better. Jean-Luc stayed on in the renovated house and interested himself more in expanses and ranges of Proust than in Molière, his two-year contract renewed yet again, and again, with still further renewals likely. He grew more handsome every year, and sometimes enjoyed a weekend with one of the many women who courted him. Sometimes a postcard came from Irène, or from Mouse and Irène, and sometimes Jean-Luc read it with interest at the table beside the pantry door where light fell in through a small window. The eighties, the nineties, seemed to be sucking him up like liquid into the future. Irène and Mouse rejoined, separated, rejoined, never with much money, travelling and working. Mouse stopped smoking and Irène followed suit. They stayed loyal lovers through the changing times. The finest lines incised themselves like invisible warpaint in Mouse's face. Irène strode from room to room, her pale eyes wheeling behind the blown lenses.

A NOTE ON THE AUTHOR

Joe Ashby Porter is the author of the novel *Eelgrass* and the two collections *The Kentucky Stories* and *Lithuania: Short Stories*. His short stories have appeared in *Antaeus, Fiction, Fiction International, Harper's, Ploughshares, Raritan, Triquarterly,* and *The Yale Review*. His fiction has been reprinted in *Best American Short Stories, The Pushcart Prize, The Store of Joys: Writers Celebrate the Fiftieth Anniversary of the N. C. Museum of Art, God: Stories, Contemporary American Fiction,* and other anthologies. His awards include two National Endowment for the Arts Creative Writing Fellowships. He has taught fiction writing at Virginia, at the Sewanee Writers' Conference, and at Duke University, where he is professor of English, and has been writer-in-residence at Brown and at the Université François Rabelais in Tours. He lives in Durham, North Carolina.